Mail Order Modiste

Book 59 in Brides of Beckham

Kirsten Osbourne

Chapter One

Cassandra Brown stood in front of the classroom, a ruler clutched firmly in her hand as she pointed to the chalkboard. Her blond hair was pulled back in a no-nonsense bun, and those piercing blue eyes scanned the room with an air of authority that kept even the most rambunctious of children in their wooden seats. The lines of multiplication tables were neat, her handwriting clear and precise on the board.

"Remember, class," Cassandra said, her voice steady and calm, "multiplication is simply repeated addition. It's not some wicked beast lurking under your beds."

One of the boys, Tommy, with freckles scattered across his nose like splattered paint, squirmed in his seat. "But Miss Brown," he piped up, "what if it is a beast, and it gobbles up all my numbers?"

The corners of Cassandra's mouth twitched ever so slightly. A moment of silence hung in the air as the children awaited her response.

"Then, Tommy," she replied, delivering the words with a deadpan delivery only a few adults might appreciate, "you shall tame it with your pencil, and ride it straight through to arithmetic victory."

A few soft chuckles bubbled through the classroom, and even Cassandra allowed the ghost of a smile to cross her face before she resumed her serious teacher's mask.

"Any other heroic quests you'd like to embark on, or can we proceed to conquer division?" she asked, though the twinkle in her eye betrayed her stern facade.

Cassandra closed the classroom door behind her, the echo of her students' laughter still lingering in the hall. She walked toward the foundling home's office, where she knew Mrs. Agatha Jackson would be buried in paperwork yet always available for a chat.

"Mrs. Jackson?" Cassandra called softly as she knocked on the open door.

"Come in, dear," Mrs. Jackson responded without looking up, her spectacles perched on the tip of her nose.

Cassandra eased into the room, taking a seat across from the woman who had been both mentor and mother figure to her. "I've been thinking," she started, her fingers fidgeting with the hem of her blouse.

"About?" Mrs. Jackson glanced up, her eyes warm and inviting.

"Teaching. It's just not...fulfilling anymore." The words tumbled out of Cassandra, her usually stoic demeanor softened by the confession.

Mrs. Jackson set her pen down and folded her hands atop the desk. "You have a heart full of dreams, Cassie. What is it that you're yearning for?"

Cassandra took a deep breath. "I want to sew, Mrs. Jackson. I want to create beautiful things. Dresses that make women feel like they are worth every penny they spend. I want to own my own dressmaking business."

"Ah," Mrs. Jackson said with a knowing smile. "I always saw how your face lit up when you worked on those costumes for the children's play. You have a magical touch with fabric and thread."

"It's the one thing that truly brings me joy," Cassandra admitted.

"Then chase that joy, my dear," Mrs. Jackson encouraged. "Why, this town could use a touch of your beauty. And who knows? Maybe your future holds more than just dresses."

Cassandra nodded, feeling a weight lift off her shoulders. "Maybe it does, Mrs. Jackson. Maybe it does."

THE CHALK SCREECHED across the blackboard as Cassandra underlined the word 'Perseverance' with a little more force than necessary. Turning to face her young audience, she caught sight of Tommy Higgins, ink pot in hand, poised to pour it over Martha's neatly plaited hair.

"Tommy Higgins!" Cassandra's voice cut through the classroom. "What do you think you're doing?"

The boy froze, guilty eyes wide and blinking. "Uh...just holdin' it, Miss Brown."

"Then I suggest you hold it over your own paper," she said, her tone brooking no argument as a few snickers erupted from his classmates.

Cassandra exhaled slowly as he reluctantly set the ink pot down. She adored the artistry of sewing, the gentle weave of fabric between her fingers, not the chaotic unpredictability of children.

After school, she sought refuge in Mrs. Jackson's office. Mrs. Jackson was cradling little Samuel, one of the foundling home's newest additions, while sorting through donations.

"Trouble with Tommy again?" Mrs. Jackson asked without looking up, her voice tender yet filled with mirth.

"Predictable as the sunrise," Cassandra sighed, leaning against the doorframe. "I swear that boy is testing me."

"Children are our most honest critics—and our toughest challenges," Mrs. Jackson said, rocking Samuel gently. "You handle him far better than you think."

"Perhaps." Cassandra smiled weakly, her heart warmed by the maternal figure before her.

"Come here, Cassie," Mrs. Jackson beckoned, patting the chair beside her.

Cassandra sat, watching as Mrs. Jackson deftly switched Samuel to her other arm. There was an effortless grace to her nurturing.

"Remember when you used to help me with the little ones' clothes? You've always had that special touch," Mrs. Jackson reminisced, a twinkle in her eye.

"Helping you was different," Cassandra admitted. "It was about creating, not corralling."

"Yet, here you are, still part of this big, noisy family." Mrs. Jackson's smile was knowing.

"Because of you," Cassandra confessed. "You gave me a place in this world."

"And you've given so much back. Don't forget that," Mrs. Jackson said softly, reaching out to squeeze Cassandra's hand.

"Thank you, Mrs. Jackson," Cassandra murmured.

"Especially then," Mrs. Jackson nodded. "Because I know, deep down, you will always carry a piece of this place with you, in the beauty you create and in the strength you show every single day."

"Thank you, Mrs. Jackson," Cassandra said, her voice thick with emotion. "For believing in me, for everything."

"Always, my dear," the matron replied, her expression earnest. "Speaking of futures," Mrs. Jackson said. "There's something I've been meaning to mention to you, Cassandra. There's a matchmaking dance next month. In Texas."

"Texas?" Cassandra echoed, caught off guard.

"Yes," Mrs. Jackson continued. "It's a grand affair, designed to unite like-minded souls. I think you'll be able to find a bachelor there who will feel the same as you do about child-rearing."

"Really?" The idea sparked an unexpected flicker of interest in Cassandra.

"Truly." Mrs. Jackson's eyes twinkled behind her spectacles. "I've been talking with Mrs. Elizabeth Tandy, and she's created this dance just for any of my girls who want to be married. It means a long train ride, and there's no guarantee you'll find someone, but I think it's worth the risk."

"Someone who understands..." Cassandra mulled over the words. The possibility of meeting a partner who shared her vision for life was an intriguing one. Perhaps this dance held more promise than just a night of frivolous entertainment.

"Think on it, dear," Mrs. Jackson said softly, giving Cassandra a reassuring pat on the shoulder before she moved away to tend to her other duties.

Cassandra watched her go, the seed of possibility planted firmly in her mind. Could Texas hold the key to her future? A partner, a dressmaking shop, a life built on shared goals rather than shared offspring. Maybe, just maybe, it was worth considering.

CASSANDRA SAT AT HER modest wooden desk as she wished she were home working on her beloved sewing machine. It had been her first purchase with her teaching money, and it was still her prized possession. The children's voices had dwindled to a chorus of whispers and rustling papers as they focused on their arithmetic. Her gaze, however, lingered not on the sums and figures chalked onto the blackboard, but out the window.

"Miss Brown?" A small voice pulled her back to the present. "Is Texas far?"

"Quite a journey from here," she replied, her eyes reflecting a daydreamer's glint. "But sometimes the furthest paths lead to the finest destinations."

"Like in your stories?" another piped up, eager for one of Miss Brown's tales.

"Exactly like in my stories." Cassandra allowed herself a small smile, then promptly directed the class back to their studies.

Later, as the children filed out with a jumble of farewells, Cassandra found herself alone with her thoughts once more. Mrs. Jackson's mention of the dance had stirred a curiosity within her that refused to be quieted. A gathering where no one expected you to dote on children? Where men didn't equate a wife's worth with her willingness to mother?

"An interesting notion, isn't it?" she mused aloud, tracing the delicate patterns of her lace collar. She pictured a man who wouldn't mind her absence from the kitchen, so long as she could create the intricate gowns that danced in her imagination.

"Miss Brown?" A voice broke her reverie. It was Mrs. Jenkins, the mother of one of Cassandra's star pupils.

"Mrs. Jenkins," Cassandra greeted her. "I was just pondering my future." She dropped her voice a bit, having long considered Mrs. Jenkins a good friend. "There will be a matchmaking dance in Texas, and I'm considering attending, and perhaps finding a man to marry."

"Are you seriously considering it?" Mrs. Jenkins asked, eyebrows raised ever so slightly above her round spectacles.

"Considering? Perhaps." Cassandra folded her hands atop her desk. "I might just find someone who shares my taste for life without the...added noise of children."

Mrs. Jenkins chuckled. "Well, if anyone can find a needle in a haystack, it's you, Cassandra."

"Especially if that haystack is filled with eligible bachelors," Cassandra quipped, her dry humor surfacing effortlessly.

"Then you'll go?"

Cassandra stood, smoothing her skirt with a steady hand. "Yes. I will attend this dance. If there is a chance to meet a man who values my dreams as much as I do—someone who would support my venture into dressmaking rather than question it—then I owe it to myself to take it." She shook her head. "And if I don't find a man, I can always get another position as a teacher there."

"Brave girl," Mrs. Jenkins said, nodding approvingly. "I hope you find the man you're looking for, and are able to start a dressmaking shop as well. I think we should all follow our dreams."

"Or at the very least, inspiration for new designs," Cassandra added.

With a heart buoyed by the prospect of fulfilling her ambitions and finding companionship on her own terms, Cassandra began to plan her journey. Texas awaited, and with it, the promise of a future tailored to her most cherished dreams.

Cassandra's fingers danced along the seam of her travel bag, tracing the careful stitches she'd placed there herself. Beside her was her sister, Deborah, with whom she'd been raised in the foundling home. There were other orphans scattered about the train, nine in total, and they traveled with Mrs. Jackson and Elizabeth Tandy, who would both help to facilitate the matches.

The rhythmic chug of the train matched her heartbeat—an eager tempo that spoke of new beginnings and ventures yet to unfold. She peered out the window at the changing landscape, each mile carrying her farther from Massachusetts and closer to the wide-open spaces of Texas.

"Never thought I'd be doing this," she murmured to Deborah, a smile tugging at the corners of her mouth. Her excitement was a living thing, coiled tight within her chest, ready to spring forth with every puff of steam that propelled the locomotive onward.

Deborah nodded. "It seems like such a foreign idea, and yet, here we are."

The train whistle blew, a forlorn cry that somehow meshed with the thrill of anticipation in Cassandra's veins. She imagined the dance, the swirl of skirts and polite nods of introduction. Her dream felt tangible now, almost within reach—a shop of her own, where the hum of her sewing machine would fill the space instead of children's voices.

Her machine was packed in the baggage car, and it was the only thing that she had of value. She couldn't bear to leave it behind.

"Last stop, ma'am," called the conductor as he passed through the car.

"Thank you," Cassandra replied, clutching her ticket like a talisman. Her legs were stiff from sitting, but they carried her off the train with purpose. The platform was abuzz with chatter and the clatter of luggage, but Cassandra walked through it all as if in a dream. She found someone to fetch her sewing machine, and then with four of her sisters, she climbed into the back of a wagon driven by Alice Dailey, the sister of Elizabeth Tandy.

Chapter Two

Andrew Forsythe wiped the sweat from his brow with a roughened hand, squinting under the relentless Texan sun. He stood in the middle of his modest ranch, surrounded by the lowing of cattle. The land stretched out before him, demanding as much as it gave, but Andrew met its challenges with the steadfast resolve of a man shaped by ambition and pragmatism.

"Another day, another chance to build something," he murmured to himself, his voice carrying on the breeze.

His dark hair, tousled by the wind, hinted at nights spent under the stars plotting the future of his enterprise. Those same gusts traced lines of labor around his eyes—deep, intense pools that seemed to absorb the very essence of the landscape before him. Even now, they surveyed his property with an unwavering gaze, missing nothing, reflecting a mind always at work.

He adjusted the brim of his hat, providing a momentary respite from the sun's glare, and turned his attention to the fence that bordered his land. He had no one working for him, and running a ranch on his own was much harder work than he'd imagined it would be. But it was worth it.

"Good fences make good neighbors," he said softly, echoing the words of some poet or other he'd once read back East.

As if in response, a stray calf bawled, straying too close to the boundary. With gentle firmness, Andrew guided it back toward the herd, his touch sure and practiced. Here, amidst the daily rhythm of ranch life, he found a contentment that filled the vast, open spaces of his heart.

"Come on, little one, back you go," he encouraged, the edges of his mouth lifting into a smile that rarely graced formal gatherings but was often shared with his four-legged charges.

Dusk began to paint the sky with strokes of orange and pink, signaling the end of another fulfilling day. Andrew took a moment to admire the view, his silhouette etched against the backdrop of a hard-earned horizon. This was his world, one where every drop of sweat and every calloused palm brought him closer to the dream he nurtured with each sunrise.

"Tomorrow," he said, his voice ripe with the quiet confidence of a man who knows the value of patience, "we'll start expanding the south pasture."

Andrew Forsythe stood at the sturdy wooden table in his modest kitchen, pressing a dough with hands that were more accustomed to roping steers than rolling pins. He chuckled to himself, the sound echoing in the empty space. Most men of the West had their share of challenges, but Andrew's were peculiar; an orphan who had grown up with little more than a name to call his own and a case of childhood mumps that left him convinced he was sterile. Yet, he carried no bitterness, only a practical acceptance that life was a series of improvised steps rather than a well-choreographed dance.

"Can't rope a steer with this," he muttered, glancing down at the pie crust that was slowly starting to resemble the map of Texas—if one squinted hard enough. The thought flickered through his mind that a companion would make such evenings as these less lonesome, someone who could turn his humble attempts at cooking into a meal worth eating.

"Sure would be nice to have a set of hands around here that knew their way around a kitchen," he said aloud, imagining a woman with a flour-dusted apron and a smile that could outshine the morning sun. Andrew wasn't a man given to fanciful daydreams, but there was something about the quiet of his kitchen that allowed for such indulgences.

"Resourceful, that's what she'd need to be," he continued. "A lady who could whip up biscuits and mend fences. Someone not afraid of a hard day's work."

He leaned back against the counter, arms crossed over his broad chest as he surveyed his work. With a wry smile, he conceded that tonight's supper would be yet another meal he would have to choke down rather than enjoy.

"Companionship," he whispered to the empty room, the word hanging in the air like a promise. It was a simple desire, rooted deep within him—a wish for someone to share in the triumphs and trials of ranch life. Someone who could laugh at the mishaps and marvel at the small victories.

"Tomorrow's another day," he said with resolve, tucking away his musings with the same care he used to store his tools.

"MORNING, BESS," ANDREW greeted the old mare as he entered the barn, the scent of hay and horse filling his nostrils. The mare nickered softly in response, her breath visible in the cool air. He patted her flank affectionately before setting about his chores.

Today, like most days, began with tending to his livestock. The clucking of chickens and the lazy oinks of pigs filled the yard as Andrew made his rounds, distributing feed with practiced ease. Each animal was more than just a source of income; they were part of the rhythm of life here.

As the sun climbed higher, Andrew turned his attention to the fence line. A few posts had seen better days, worn by time and weather. He set to work with hammer and nails. With every strike, he fortified not only his property but also his future, every repaired slat a testament to his resolve.

"Sturdy as ever," he muttered, admiring his handiwork.

"Looks like you'll hold up for another season," he said to the fence. He wiped his brow and cast a glance back at the expanse of land he called his own. It was a simple life, but it was his, built from the ground up with nothing but determination and a dream.

"Tomorrow's another day," Andrew reaffirmed to himself, a smile playing on his lips as he took in the rustic charm of his world.

Andrew squinted up at the vast Texas sky, shielding his eyes from the afternoon sun with a dusty palm. His gaze traced the outline of the horizon where his land met the heavens—a boundary he was determined to push.

"More cattle, more acres," he murmured to himself, the words a personal creed. He had plans sketched out in the ledger back in his modest ranch house. It was full of figures and diagrams that spoke of ambition beyond his current means. Yet, the tightness of coin did little to dampen Andrew's spirit.

"Can't let a little drought of dollars dry up the dream," he chuckled, the sound carried away by a warm breeze that rustled through the nearby mesquite trees.

He strode across the field, boots crunching on the dry earth, his mind bustling with thoughts of windmills and water troughs that could one day dot this landscape. He was building a legacy, piece by painstaking piece.

Pausing beside the corral, Andrew leaned on the weathered wooden rail, watching his small herd grazing. The cattle were a start, but he envisioned them multiplied tenfold. "Won't be long, ladies," he promised the oblivious animals, a whisper of laughter in his voice.

In the quiet that followed, Andrew's thoughts turned inward. He knew the kind of partner he needed by his side—someone who understood the value of dawn till dusk labor, who could match his entrepreneurial zeal with a steady hand and a shared vision.

"Someone to build with me," he said to the emptiness around him. Such a woman would be as rare as rain in this sunbaked land, yet Andrew believed she existed. She had to.

"Companionship...That's the true expansion I need," he confided to the sprawling oaks that lined the edge of his property, their branches swaying as if in agreement.

AT CHURCH ON SUNDAY, he mentioned his need for companionship to a friend.

"There's going to be a dance," Aaron said. "Here at the church. Someone is bringing some orphans from the east, and any bachelors are welcome to go. Catch is, we're expected to marry them the night of the dance if we want to keep them."

Andrew stared at Aaron for a moment. "Are you serious?"

Aaron nodded. "Sure am. I'm going to be there."

"As will I. When will it happen again?"

Aaron gave him the details, and Andrew left church that morning with his eyes full of hope. He was going to find a bride...one who wouldn't mind that he was incapable of fathering children.

ANDREW PATTED THE FLANK of his favorite mare, a comfort in the routine. He allowed himself a smile as he filled the troughs, the water splashing rhythmically—a sound as reassuring as the chorus of cicadas come dusk. This was a life of challenge, each day unfurling with the steadfast certainty of hard work and the rewards it reaped.

"Easy there, Bess," he murmured, the mare nuzzling into his palm for an affectionate scratch. "We're doing just fine, you and I."

He stepped back, surveying his handiwork. The fence mended, the stable tidy, every task checked off his mental list with a nod of satisfaction. Life on the ranch offered little in the way of luxury, but Andrew reveled in its simplicities—the warmth of the sun, the strength in his muscles, the peace of solitude. Yet, even as contentment settled over him like evening's first cool breeze, he knew the picture wasn't complete.

"Of course, a pair of hands to share the load wouldn't go amiss," he said to Bess, who seemed content to listen. "Someone to stoke the fire and bring life to this old house." His thoughts drifted to a partner, a woman with grit and grace, her laughter mingling with the wind.

"Maybe she'll love the land like I do," he continued, half to himself, "and won't shy away from a day's work. We'd be partners, in truth. Her success mine, and mine hers."

With the sun hanging low, casting long shadows across the land, Andrew leaned against the corral. A soft sigh escaped him as he watched the horizon, where earth met sky in a promise of tomorrow.

"Could be she's out there right now," he whispered, the hint of a dream coloring his words, "waiting for a man who needs more than just a cook or a pretty face by the hearth."

The thought brought a chuckle, light and unforced. It was a comforting notion, imagining someone willing to roll up her sleeves and take on the world beside him. And why not? This was 1898, after all—times were changing, and so were the roles of men and women on the frontier.

"Yup," he said, pushing off from the fence with a new resolve, "she'll be as fierce as the land, and together, we'll tame it."

Andrew hoisted a sack of feed over his shoulder, the muscles in his arms flexing under the strain. He poured the contents into the trough and patted the flank of his nearest horse, the sturdy creature blowing warm air from its nostrils in quiet appreciation.

"Supper time, Bess," he said, a grin spreading across his face. The mare nickered softly, nosing at the feed as if to thank him.

Turning away from the stable, Andrew's gaze wandered to the open plains beyond his property. The expanse seemed to echo with possibilities, each rolling hill a whisper of potential futures. As he stood there, a sense of anticipation bubbled up inside him, lifting the corners of his lips into a hopeful smile.

"Maybe it's about time I stopped being so darn practical," he mused aloud, considering the notion of love and companionship. "Might be nice to have someone to share all this with." The idea of another mouth to feed was a bit scary, but he was sure he could make it work.

"Tomorrow's another day," he said, a spark of excitement in his dark eyes as he walked back toward his modest home. There was work to be done before nightfall, yet his thoughts strayed to softer things: laughter shared under the stars, hands clasped tight while forging ahead together.

As he reached the porch, Andrew paused, looking back at the land he had dedicated himself to. His heart was full, not just of dreams for his ranch, but for the life he might build upon it.

"Who knows?" he whispered to the twilight, allowing himself to indulge in the fantasy for just a moment longer. "She could be closer than I think."

With that thought warming him against the evening chill, Andrew stepped inside. He lit a lamp, its glow steady and strong, much like his resolve. Tomorrow held no guarantees, but it did hold promise—the promise of growth, of love, and of shared victories.

"Good things are coming," he assured himself, the words a simple prayer. And with that, he settled down for the night, content in the knowledge that each new dawn brought him one step closer to the future he yearned for—a future where hard work wasn't just rewarded with prosperity, but with a partner to call his own.

Chapter Three

After spending a night at Susan Dailey's house, it was time for the big dance, which was the true reason they were in Texas, though Cassie had enjoyed the travel and the ability to see a new place. Before they had left the train station in Beckham, Cassie had never been outside of Massachusetts.

Cassie stepped into the church for the dance, her heart pounding. The church was alive with the sounds of laughter and conversations. She felt a tingle of excitement at the prospect of meeting someone special, yet a knot of nervousness tightened in her stomach, as if she were about to face a room of rowdy schoolchildren rather than potential suitors.

Across the room, amidst the jovial chaos of hopeful hearts and eager glances, stood a man whose presence seemed to command the space around him. His eyes scanned the room not with the hunger of a man in desperate search of a partner, but with the quiet confidence of one who knew his worth and was calculating his next move.

He leaned against a wooden pillar, arms folded across his chest, his posture relaxed yet undeniably alert—a rancher surveying his land with an eye for opportunity. Cassie noted the subtle crease in his brow, the way his gaze lingered thoughtfully on the different women before moving on, as if he were envisioning a future and pondering the pieces needed to complete it. And though they were but strangers in a crowded room filled with festive noise, Cassie felt drawn to the man.

Cassie's nerves settled into a simmering curiosity as she moved through the crowd, her gaze inadvertently returning to the man by the pillar. Their eyes met, and for a fleeting moment, the clamorous room seemed to hush around them. Andy's lips curled into a knowing smirk, mirroring the half-smile that tugged at Cassie's mouth. It was a silent exchange, but it spoke volumes—a shared recognition that they were both outsiders observing the dance.

Taking a steadying breath, Cassie navigated closer, her blue eyes locking onto his dark ones with an unspoken challenge. With each step, the hum of fiddles and the rhythm of boots on wood faded into the background.

"I'm Cassandra Brown," she said, voice steady but laced with a playful undertone.

"Miss Brown," Andy replied. "Andrew Forsythe. My friends call me Andy." He paused for a moment as if studying her. "You look positively thrilled to be here."

"Thrilled is...one word for it," Cassie quipped, her lips quirking upward. "I find the concept of dancing in circles only to end up right where you started rather perplexing."

"Agreed," he nodded. "Much like the idea of raising children, don't you think? An endless waltz of noise and mess, and for what?"

"Very true." She chuckled, the sound surprising even herself. "A life of servitude to small tyrants does not appeal to me in the slightest."

"Nor to me," Andy confessed, his smile widening. "I've often thought my ambitions are more suited to cattle than to cradles."

"Fortunate, then, that cows rarely require schooling or diaper changes," Cassie remarked, pleased by his company and the ease of their banter. "I happen to know what's in those diapers, and I have no desire to be around them."

"Very fortunate," Andy agreed, his eyes gleaming with mirth. "I daresay we share an uncommon perspective, Miss Brown."

"Uncommon, yet refreshingly practical, Mr. Forsythe." Cassie's heart fluttered at the thought that perhaps she wasn't alone in her preferences after all. She'd stumbled upon a kindred spirit in the middle of a dance meant to match orphaned women with lonely men. Andy Forsythe wasn't just another rancher looking for a wife to fill his homestead with children. He was like her, content with a life untouched by the pitter-patter of little feet.

"Never thought I'd meet someone who shared my sentiments," Cassie mused, her gaze fixed on Andy's face, searching for any sign of jest. Instead, she found only genuine agreement.

"Neither did I," Andy admitted with a soft chuckle. "Most around these parts see marriage and children as the same—a package deal."

"An expensive package," Cassie added with a wry smile, feeling an unfamiliar sense of camaraderie bloom within her chest. It was a relief, a validation of her own choices. Not everyone longed for the patter of tiny hands and feet—some were content with quieter, simpler dreams.

"True," Andy said, his dark eyes reflecting a depth that beckoned her to look closer. "I suppose it's all moot for me anyway." His voice lowered, a thread of vulnerability woven through his words. "I had the mumps as a child. Doctor said it left me...well, unlikely to father children."

His candidness struck a chord in Cassie, urging her to share her own truth. "I understand more than you might think, Mr. Forsythe. Teaching in Massachusetts...it opened my eyes. I realized motherhood isn't where my heart lies."

"Miss Brown..." Andy's gaze held hers, his expression gentle. "Cassie, that's not something many would admit."

"Nor is your situation," she countered, empathy warming her tone. "Yet here we are, two people who are willing to go against what society considers the norm."

"Seems so." He reached for a glass of punch from a nearby table and offered it to her. As their fingers brushed, a current of unspoken understanding passed between them.

"Thank you," she whispered, her hand trembling slightly as she accepted the drink. The conversation had shifted, no longer just idle chatter but something raw and real. They were peeling back layers, revealing truths that others might shy away from, and it drew them closer in the most unexpected way.

"Thank you," she repeated, not just for the punch, but for the moment—for the connection that neither of them had anticipated, yet both desperately needed.

Cassie's hand was still tingling from the touch of Andy's fingers on hers. She sipped the punch, its sweetness on her tongue mirroring the unexpected joy bubbling in her chest. Her eyes locked with his once more, and she found herself teetering on the edge of a wild idea.

"Mr. Forsythe," she began, her voice a mix of mischief and boldness, "if neither of us is inclined to raise children, and both of us are seeking companionship..."

Andy's dark eyes sparkled with the same adventurous glint she felt lighting up her own. "Miss Brown, are you suggesting what I think you're suggesting?"

Cassie set down the glass with a decisive clink. "I am. Perhaps we should consider a partnership of a different sort. Marriage but without a desire for children, to aid your ranch and my dream of dressmaking. What do you say?"

He didn't hesitate, his confident demeanor only amplifying the allure of the impromptu proposal. "I say, let's not waste time. Cassie, will you be my wife?"

Her breath hitched. It was madness, sheer madness, but thrilling too. "Yes, Andy. I will."

"Friends and neighbors!" he called out, causing a lull as curious faces turned toward the pair. "Miss Cassandra Brown has agreed to become my wife!"

For a moment the room was silent, but then a young woman Andy had never met began clapping and was soon joined by the others.

Cassie grinned at her sister of the heart, Deborah and nodded slowly. "That's my sister, Deborah," she whispered to Andy.

"Right now?" someone called out.

"Right now," Andy confirmed, his hand finding Cassie's and squeezing it with unspoken promises of shared tomorrows.

As lanterns cast a golden glow over the dance floor, Cassie twirled in Andy's arms, her laughter mingling with the lively tune of the fiddle. Her blue eyes sparkled with mischief as she caught the rhythm. Andy's eyes were filled with laughter, his confident steps guiding her through the sea of dancers who now viewed them not just as partners for the evening, but partners in life.

"Seems we're quite the spectacle," Andy mused, his voice a low hum above the music.

"Let them look," Cassie replied, her words bold and carefree. "We've nothing to hide."

Their smiles were twin crescents of sheer delight, unspoken understanding knitting them closer with every beat of the drum. The crowd parted for them, giving space to the couple that had so suddenly become one. And in that expanse, they danced as though the world had shrunk to the size of the wooden planks beneath their feet.

Time slipped by, marked only by the changing tempo of the songs. The stars outside began their slow arc, winking at the newly betrothed as if to bless the union that had taken root under their watchful eyes.

"Guess we need to go and find the preacher now," Andy said later, as they paused for a breath, leaning against the punch table.

"Sounds good to me." She looked around. "They said there would be one here so we could marry on the spot."

"Well, I saw Amos Kauffman a bit ago. He's our preacher. We should go and talk to him."

"That sounds like a brilliant plan."

"The fact that you recognize my brilliance makes you so much more in my eyes than you were a moment ago."

"I thought you were already entranced by my charming wit?" she teased.

"Oh, I was," he said with a laugh.

They made their way through the throng of dancers and found Amos Kauffman deep in conversation with Hannah, one of Cassie's sisters who had come to Texas with her. "Can we get married now?" Andy asked Amos.

Amos looked confused for a moment, but then he turned his full attention to Andy and Cassandra. "Of course." There, with people dancing behind them, they went through the ceremony, and Amos pronounced them man and wife.

Andy leaned down and brushed a soft kiss against Cassie's lips. Hannah stepped forward and hugged her sister. "I hope you find all the happiness you deserve," Hannah whispered.

"And you," Cassie said softly. "Are you certain you know what you're doing spending time with a pastor this way?"

Hannah shook her head. "No, I think I may have lost my mind. But he's the one..."

"Ready to step into a new adventure?" Andy's voice cut through the whispered conversation between the sisters.

"Only if you are," Cassie responded, her blue eyes reflecting a mixture of daring and wonder.

"Then it's settled." He offered his arm, and she took it, her grip firm and sure.

"Quite the leap we've taken, Mr. Forsythe," Cassie murmured, allowing herself a small, hopeful smile.

"Leaps are easier when you've got the right person by your side, Mrs. Forsythe." His dark eyes crinkled at the corners with a smile to match hers.

They moved toward the exit, their steps slow and measured, as if they were both aware that each footfall was taking them closer to an unknown destiny. The warm night air greeted them, and they paused at the threshold, looking out into the dark expanse that held their future.

"Never thought I'd find myself here," Cassie confessed, squeezing his arm lightly.

"Life has a funny way of surprising us," Andy replied, gazing down at her with a warmth that made her heart flutter.

"Indeed, it does," she whispered back, leaning into him slightly, feeling the strength of his presence.

With a deep breath, they stepped out into the night together, the door closing behind them with a soft click. The anticipation of what lay ahead hung between them. Cassie felt for the first time that her future was filled with love and promise. It felt good.

Andy drove them to the small home he'd built, and he waited to hear something negative about it. It wasn't the home he'd dreamed of, and he was sure it wasn't the home she'd always wanted, but it was theirs.

He sent her inside while he unhitched the horses.

Cassie wandered into the house and looked around, realizing it was all basically one room, but she didn't mind. There was a kitchen area, a space for sitting, and a bed. What more did she need? Back in Massachusetts, she'd shared the floor with some of the other young women who were too old to take up the precious beds meant for the children.

When Andy joined her, she smiled at him. "It's perfect."

He gaped at her for a moment, but then smiled, enfolding her in his arms. "It's a perfect place to start," he agreed.

Chapter Four

Cassandra and Andrew stood hesitantly before the bed, the reality of their wedding night sending a thrill of anticipation tinged with nervousness through them both.

"Shall we...?" Andy's voice trailed off, his dark eyes seeking hers for consent.

Cassie nodded, her heart fluttering like the wings of a trapped sparrow. She watched as Andy's hands fumbled with the buttons of his shirt, the normally steady fingers betraying his unfamiliarity with this most intimate of moments.

"Here, let me," Cassie said, her hands surprisingly steady as she helped him. The fabric parted to reveal the solid chest she had only imagined under the layers of clothes he wore during the day.

"Thank you," he murmured, his lips curving into a shy smile that made her feel at ease, despite the circumstances.

Together, they discovered the rhythm of each other's bodies, awkward at first but soon moving together in a dance that felt ancient. Laughter mingled with soft sighs, the sound sweeter than any symphony to their ears as they embraced the newness of marriage.

MORNING LIGHT PEEKED through the curtains when Cassie woke. Andy still slept, his breath steady and even. Slipping from the bed, she dressed quickly and tiptoed to the kitchen. She set about making breakfast, cracking eggs into a bowl. She'd made more meals than she could count, something that had been part of the learning of all the female orphans at the foundling home.

By the time Andy came in, wiping his hands on his trousers after milking the cows and collecting eggs, the smells of cooking filled the small house.

"Good morning," Cassie greeted him, setting a plate of scrambled eggs and bacon in front of him.

"Morning, Cassie." Andy's voice was gruff with sleep, but his smile was wide. "This looks wonderful. I have to admit, I wasn't thinking about marriage bringing me better meals until just this second."

As they ate, Cassie ventured into the silence with her dream, "I've been thinking...I'd like to start a dressmaker's shop. I love to sew, and I design dresses for my friends. I'm very good."

Andy paused, his fork mid-air. "That's a fine idea, Cassie. A real fine idea."

"Really?" She looked up, hope etching her features.

"Of course. You're a talented seamstress, and it would be good for us—good for the ranch."

"I didn't know if..."

"Listen," he interrupted gently. "If you want to start building up clients, you should do it. And I'll make you a small separate room for your work. How does that sound?"

"Perfect," Cassie breathed, her heart soaring. The simple breakfast suddenly tasted like the finest feast, and the future seemed brighter than she had imagined it ever could.

ANDY HOISTED THE LAST hay bale onto the wagon, his muscles burning pleasantly with the effort. As he straightened up and wiped the sweat from his brow, his thoughts wandered to Cassie. He chuckled to himself, thinking how different she was from the women he'd known before—serious about her work, sure, but with a dry sense of humor that caught him off guard. And she didn't want children. A rare thing for a woman in these parts, but it suited Andy just fine. The fact that Cassie shared his disinterest in parenthood felt like a stroke of luck.

"Good fortune indeed," he muttered to himself, a grin spreading across his face. With his dream of expanding the ranch and Cassie's of opening her own dressmaker's shop, they were set to be quite the team.

Inside the house, Cassie hummed a tune while she swept the already spotless floor. The early morning light streamed through the windows, casting warm patches on the wooden planks. She imagined every corner of their home filled with rolls of fabric, the chatter of satisfied customers, and the steady rhythm of her sewing machine.

"First things first," she said aloud, setting the broom aside and surveying the tidy room. "I need my sewing machine from Susan's." Her mind whirred with plans as she thought about a piece of fabric she had brought along when they'd come from Massachusetts. It was a lovely shade of blue, one that made her eyes stand out even more.

"Imagine wearing a dress of my own creation to church," she thought, the idea blooming in her mind like wildflowers in spring. "I'll make myself a dress, and everyone will see what I can do."

She pictured the admiring glances and the whispers of inquiry, the potential orders that might follow. Cassie could almost hear the snip of her scissors and the whisper of the fabric as she cut into it, creating something beautiful and desired.

"Then they'll come, one by one, eager for a dress of their own," she whispered with determination. "And my dream won't be just a dream any longer."

CASSIE SET THE PLATES down with a clink, her hands steady despite the flutter in her chest. Across the table, Andy paused, his spoon halfway to his mouth. The savory aroma of stew filled the modest kitchen as the golden light of sunset spilled through the window, bathing everything in a warm glow.

"Andy," Cassie began, her voice soft but sure, "I've been thinking about how I want to start my business."

He chewed slowly, then set his fork down, his dark eyes meeting hers with interest. "Tell me more," he said, the corners of his mouth lifting into an encouraging smile.

With each detail she shared, Andy's smile widened. "Cassie, that's a good idea. Let's fetch your machine from Susan's tonight."

The ride to the Daileys' house was filled with talk of patterns and fabrics, the wagon bouncing along the dusty road as stars began to dot the evening sky.

Upon arrival, they were greeted by the scent of fresh cookies wafting from the kitchen. Susan stood in the doorway, her blond hair catching the last of the daylight, green eyes sparkling with warmth.

"Come in, you two! We've just made tea," Susan called out, ushering them inside.

Once settled at the Daileys' sturdy kitchen table, surrounded by the chatter of family life, Cassie took a deep breath and launched into her plans.

"Susan, I want to create dresses for the women around here. To give them something special, something just theirs."

Susan reached for a cookie, her gaze never leaving Cassie. "That sounds marvelous, Cassie. Did you make the dress you're wearing?"

Cassie nodded. "I did. But I made this out of two old dresses that came to the orphanage. I can do much better when I'm starting with a fresh piece of fabric."

Cassie unfolded the fabric across the kitchen table, its cornflower blue hue dancing under the soft glow of the oil lamp. Susan's eyes lit up as she ran her fingers over the material, the corners of her mouth turning upward.

"Blue always was my favorite," Susan mused, her gaze shifting from the cloth to Cassie's face. "I think a dress in this would be perfect for church on Sunday. Can you have it done by then?"

"I'm sure I can," Cassie replied, her voice steady with confidence. She retrieved her tape measure, a tool that had become an extension of her hand, and began taking Susan's measurements, noting each number with care. It would be so much better to have Susan wear the dress, but she would be sad to part with the beautiful blue fabric.

"Your stitches are like tiny works of art, Cassie," Susan said, standing still as Cassie worked around her. "I'll be the envy of every lady at service."

Cassie offered a small, satisfied smile, imagining Susan parading in the dress, a walking advertisement for her business.

Later that night, after the wagon ride home beneath a blanket of stars, Cassie and Andy entered their modest homestead, the air between them charged with a new sense of purpose. They quietly prepared for bed, anticipation building with each passing moment.

As they lay together, Andy traced the outline of Cassie's face with his fingertips, the touch featherlight and full of adoration. "I'm glad about us, Cassie," he whispered, his dark eyes reflecting the moonlight streaming through the window. "Glad we don't have to worry about children. Just us, and whatever life we build."

"Me too, Andy," Cassie responded, her heart swelling with a mixture of relief and love. "Just us." She was surprised at how close she already felt to this man who she'd just met the previous evening. She never would have imagined that a good marriage could come from meeting someone the way she did, but she wasn't about to complain. He was a good man, and they would be happy together.

Entwined in each other's arms, they found solace in their shared understanding, their love growing stronger in the quiet spaces of the night.

Cassie nestled into the crook of Andy's arm, her breathing slow and even, as her mind spun with a whirlwind of emotions and plans swirling in her mind.

"Goodnight," Andy murmured, his voice low and comforting, like the distant rumble of thunder on a clear night.

"Goodnight," she whispered back, feeling the rise and fall of his chest against her cheek. Her thoughts fluttered to the dress she would soon create for Susan, the stitches and seams already forming in her imagination.

In the quiet haven of their home, with moonlight spilling across the quilted bedspread, Cassie allowed herself to dream beyond the homestead. She envisioned women from all around, drawn to her skillful hands, each one leaving with a piece of her artistry—a dress, a blouse, perhaps even a fancy skirt or apron.

Cassie's last conscious thought was a silent promise to herself and to the life she was building. She was going to make it, she was sure of it. And with that certainty warming her from the inside out, Cassandra drifted off to sleep, her dreams as bright and promising as the dawn that would soon break over the rolling hills of their land.

Chapter Five

Cassie's fingers were a blur as she added the final touches to Susan's dress. The hum of her sewing machine mixed with the sizzling sound from the stove where a pot of stew simmered. Though cooking was a pleasure, the dress commanded her attention. Cassie snipped the last thread and held up the finished garment.

"Land sakes, it's done," she murmured to herself, admiring the delicate lace trim and the way the skirt would twirl.

The next day dawned clear and bright, with a promise carried on the gentle breeze. Cassie and Andy stood at Susan's door, the dress carefully draped over Cassie's arm. Susan's green eyes were sparkling with anticipation as she opened the door.

"Is that it?" Susan clasped her hands together, nodding toward the dress.

"I finished last night," Cassie replied, unfolding the dress for Susan to see.

"Let me try it on!" Susan disappeared, her blond curls bouncing as she moved.

When she emerged, the dress fit like a glove, hugging her figure in all the right places. She twirled, and the skirt fanned out beautifully.

"David, look!" Susan called, beaming.

David turned from where he'd been quietly conversing with Andy. His face softened, his eyes lighting up as he took in his wife's appearance. "Susan," he said, "you're as lovely as the day I met you."

"Oh, David!" Susan rushed over, her cheeks flushed with pleasure. She wrapped her arms around him, and they shared a moment that seemed to hold all the tenderness of their years together.

"Thank you, Cassie," Susan said, turning back to Cassie with a grateful look. "This dress...it's more than I dreamed."

Cassie nodded, feeling a swell of satisfaction. "I'm just glad you like it."

"Like it? I love it!" Susan's laugh rang out, clear and joyful. "I can't wait to show everyone at church!"

As they left Susan's house, Cassie caught David's eye. He nodded to her, an unspoken thanks passing between them.

Cassie's fingers closed around the crinkled bills Susan had pressed into her palm. With a spring in her step, she got down from the wagon, thrilled to finally earn money for doing what she loved best. The fabric store was a canvas of colors and textures, and she chose with care, selecting bolts that whispered promises of gowns yet to be born.

"At least four dresses," she murmured to herself, satisfaction lacing her tone as the shopkeeper tallied up her purchase. "This is just the start." With the extra fabric, she could make some dresses for little girls, or save what was left for a quilt. Oh, the possibilities were endless.

"Looks like you've got quite the project ahead," the shopkeeper said, eyeing the pile of fabric with a knowing smile.

"I do," Cassie replied, her mind already racing with designs as she handed over the payment. "A very exciting one. I'm going to start my own business making dresses."

The man pursed his lips. "If you make any you can't sell, people are always looking for ready-made dresses. I'd be happy to sell them for you."

Cassie smiled. "Thank you. I'll keep that in mind!"

Leaving the store with her arms full, Cassie could almost see the future stitches aligning under her hands, each piece of cloth transforming into something treasured.

Back at the ranch, Andy waited for her with a gentle smile, his dark eyes reflecting a silent question about her trip to town. She nodded, her smile an answer enough, and they set out across the sprawling expanse of their shared land.

"Over there's where I have the cattle grazing now, but I'll be moving them soon," Andy began, pointing to the distant fields where dots of moving brown hinted at the bovine occupants. "And that's the vegetable patch. Won't find fresher produce anywhere."

"Everything's so...alive," Cassie remarked, her gaze sweeping over the vibrant greenery.

"Wait till you see the stables," Andy said with a hint of pride in his voice.

Andy introduced her to each horse with a fondness that spoke of deep bonds formed through care and respect.

"This here is Bess," he said, patting a chestnut mare with a white blaze running down her nose. "She's the gentlest soul you'll ever meet."

"Hello, Bess," Cassie smiled, extending her hand tentatively, delighted when the horse nuzzled into it. The warmth of the animal's breath against her skin was oddly comforting.

"Each one has their quirks, but they're all part of the ranch's heart," Andy explained, guiding her through the nuances of equine care. "Lots to learn, but I think you'll get the hang of it."

"I can't wait to get to know them all," Cassie said, her excitement obvious.

"You're going to love them all as much as I do," Andy replied, the corner of his mouth lifting in a half-smile that told her he truly believed it.

CASSIE'S FINGERS TRACED the fresh patterns etched onto the fabric, her blue eyes dancing with visions of dresses yet to be born. "I can't wait to get started," she said, her voice bubbling over with enthusiasm. "It's been a dream for so long, and now it's finally happening."

Andy leaned against the doorframe, his dark eyes following her movements with quiet pride. "You've got talent and determination," he said, the hint of a grin tugging at his lips. "Why not set up shop right here? A place where you can work and meet your customers."

"Here?" Cassie paused, considering the idea. She glanced around the homestead, her gaze settling on a sun-kissed patch of land near the house.

"Right there," Andy pointed, stepping beside her. "Close to the house, easy for folks to find."

"Perfect," she agreed, a flush of excitement warming her cheeks.

The very next morning, Andy rounded up a pile of lumber and a toolbox full of well-worn tools. His hands, strong from years of ranching, picked up a saw as if it were an extension of himself.

"Hand me that hammer, will you?" he asked, nodding toward the tool bench.

"Of course." Cassie passed him the hammer, their fingers brushing briefly in the exchange—a simple touch that sent a shared spark between them.

Together, they measured and cut, the rhythmic thud of the hammer mingling with the soft creak of bending wood. Cassie held each board steady as Andy drove in the nails, their teamwork seamless.

"Seems we make quite the pair," Cassie remarked, a playful note in her voice.

"Knew we would," Andy replied without missing a beat, his smile genuine.

They worked side by side, the hours slipping by unnoticed. Laughter echoed through the air, punctuated by the occasional shout when a stubborn nail refused to go in straight.

"Stubborn as a mule, this one," Cassie joked, wiggling the bent nail.

"Let me at it," Andy chuckled, taking the nail from her and setting it right with a few deft swings.

THE SHOP STOOD PROUDLY next to the house. Cassie stepped inside, her blue eyes scanning the space that was now hers to fill. She inhaled the scent of fresh lumber and earth, a smile dancing on her lips.

"Right then," she murmured to herself as she set about organizing bolts of colorful fabric on the wooden shelves Andy had built into the walls. Each bolt was placed with care, the vibrant hues a promise of creations yet to come.

Her sewing machine found its place by the window where the light was generous. With each turn of the screw and adjustment of the needle, Cassie's dream stitched itself more firmly into reality.

She hummed a tune, one that had often soothed the children back at the foundling home when their spirits needed lifting. Now, it lifted her own as she hung her only finished dress on the wall. It twirled gently in the breeze, as if it too was celebrating this new beginning.

"Knock, knock." The familiar voice pulled Cassie from her thoughts.

"Come in, Andy," Cassie called without turning, knowing he'd enter with that easy stride of his.

Andy stepped through the doorway, something large and artfully concealed behind his back. His dark eyes gleamed with a mix of pride and mischief.

"Got a little something for you," he said, revealing a beautifully crafted sewing table. Its wood was smooth and polished, the legs carved with delicate flourishes that spoke of hours spent in meticulous labor.

Cassie's hands flew to her mouth, her heart swelling. "Andy, it's...it's wonderful."

"Thought you might need a proper place to bring those dresses to life," he replied, setting the table down in the heart of the shop.

"Thank you," Cassie breathed out, placing her hands atop the table and feeling the love that had gone into its making.

She looked up at him, her eyes shining. "I can't wait to start my first project here."

"Nor can I wait to see it," Andy said, his voice carrying a note of admiration that wrapped around her like a warm shawl.

Cassie sat at the new sewing table, its surface alive with scattered fabric swatches and sketched designs. She held a pencil delicately between her fingers, drawing lines that flowed into the shapes of gowns and frocks.

"What are you thinking for this one?" Andy leaned over her shoulder, his dark eyes curious as he pointed at a sketch of a summer dress. "Something light?"

"Exactly," Cassie said, nodding. "A soft cotton, maybe with little floral patterns. Perfect for the warm weather."

"Sounds lovely," Andy replied, his interest genuine. He wasn't a man of many words, but when it came to her work, he always had something encouraging to say.

"Thanks," she smiled, selecting a bolt of fabric in a delicate shade of blue. "This one will do nicely."

Outside the window, Andy returned to the vastness of their land, his figure growing smaller as he moved farther away. The sun beat down on his back while he checked the cattle, ensuring they were well-fed and content. His days were long, filled with the tasks required to keep the ranch running—from mending broken fences to mapping out expansion plans.

"Need any help with that fence later?" Cassie called out as Andy passed by the shop again, a toolbox in hand.

"Got it under control, but thanks!" Andy's voice carried back to her, steady and sure.

"All right then," she murmured to herself, her hands deftly laying out the pattern pieces onto the fabric, ready to be cut.

CASSIE SET THE DINNER table with a simple grace, placing utensils next to plates heaped with steaming roasted chicken and fresh vegetables from the garden. The aroma filled the cozy kitchen, promising warmth and nourishment after a day's hard work. Andy walked in just as she was pouring two glasses of water, his dark hair tousled from the wind outside.

"Something smells heavenly," Andy said, his eyes lighting up at the sight of the meal.

"Your favorite," Cassie replied, her blue eyes twinkling. "I figured you'd be famished after wrangling fences all day."

"Can't argue with that logic," he chuckled, taking his seat. They ate in comfortable silence for a few moments, savoring the food and each other's company.

"Your new dress design," Andy began, breaking the quiet with genuine curiosity, "how's it coming along?"

"Better than I hoped," Cassie answered with a satisfied smile. "I think the ladies in town will adore the lace trimmings."

"Can't wait to see it. Maybe you'll start a fashion revolution out here," he teased, winking at her.

"Perhaps," Cassie laughed, shaking her head at the thought. "But only if you manage to turn this ranch into the empire you're dreaming of."

"Sounds like a plan to me," Andy said, reaching across the table to give her hand a quick squeeze.

Their laughter faded into the soft clinking of cutlery as they finished their meal. When the last bite was taken, they lingered at the table, neither in a rush to return to their separate tasks.

"Speaking of dreams," Cassie ventured cautiously, "we need to talk about how we're handling things around here."

"Sure thing," Andy nodded, giving her his full attention. "What's on your mind?"

"Well, I can manage the dressmaking just fine," Cassie started, "but I want to make sure you don't feel like I'm neglecting...us."

"Hey now," Andy interjected gently, "you took on a big challenge, and you're doing great. As for me and the ranch," he said, "we're holding up just fine. We're partners, Cassie, remember? In business and in life."

"Partners," she said, the word solidifying something deep within her. "So we're agreed then? You focus on the cattle and the land, and I'll take care of the dresses and our home."

"Agreed," Andy confirmed. "And we help each other out whenever needed. That's what marriage is about, right?"

"Right," Cassie affirmed, warmth spreading through her at the solidity of their arrangement.

CASSIE TUGGED AT ANDY'S hand, a fresh breeze playing with the loose strands of her blond hair. "Let's take a break," she said, eyes twinkling. "The prairie won't go anywhere."

"All right then, if you say so." Andy replied, his voice carrying a hint of amusement.

They left the hum of the sewing machine and the creaking of the ranch gates behind, stepping into the vast expanse of wildflowers and tall grasses. As they walked, their hands remained intertwined, anchoring them in silent companionship. The sun cast a warm glow on the landscape, turning the distant mountains into silhouettes of pure gold.

"Look there," Cassie pointed toward a cluster of deer grazing near a stream, her blue eyes reflecting the simple beauty of the moment.

Andy followed her gaze, nodding appreciatively. "This land...it's something else."

"Sure is," Cassie agreed, squeezing his hand gently.

The tranquility of the countryside wrapped around them like a quilt, stitching the moments of peace into the fabric of their relationship. With each step, they found common rhythms and shared smiles that spoke volumes of their deepening connection.

One afternoon when dark clouds gathered with startling swiftness, they hurried back to find the shop taking the brunt of the storm's fury.

"Goodness!" Cassie exclaimed, surveying the damage. A portion of the roof had given way, and water was already pooling on the floor.

"Nothing we can't fix," Andy assured her, rolling up his sleeves. "You and me, we're tougher than a little rain."

Together, they worked through the evening, patching up the roof with spare shingles and mopping up the water. Their movements were efficient and practiced - a dance they'd unknowingly choreographed over time.

"Can't believe how quickly that storm came up," Cassie remarked, wiping her brow.

"Nature's full of surprises," Andy replied, hammering the last nail into place. "But so are we."

"Seems like it," she chuckled, watching him work.

A FEW DAYS LATER, A customer arrived with demands that would test any saint's patience. The woman poked at the dresses on display, her nose wrinkled in distaste.

"Are these the latest styles?" she asked, dubious.

"Yes, they are," Cassie responded, maintaining her composure. "I can assure you they're very fashionable in Boston."

"Seems I expected too much," the woman sighed, turning away.

"Ma'am," Andy interjected smoothly, "perhaps there's something specific you have in mind? Cassie's quite talented. She can craft just about anything."

Cassie shot him a grateful glance and took over, guiding the woman through fabric choices and potential designs. By the end, they'd sketched out a dress that left the customer more than satisfied.

"Thank you," Cassie whispered to Andy as the woman left, a spring in her step.

"Anytime," he winked. "Partners, remember?"

"Right," Cassie replied, her heart light despite the challenges. "Partners."

The wooden planks of the porch creaked gently as Cassie settled into the rocking chair beside Andy.

"Beautiful, isn't it?" she murmured, her blue eyes reflecting the vibrant colors of the sunset.

"Sure is," Andy agreed, his dark eyes not on the sunset but on her. "But not as beautiful as the life we're building here."

Cassie smiled, tucking a loose strand of blond hair behind her ear. "It's hard to believe how much has changed," she said, thinking of the bustling dress shop and the thriving ranch around them.

"Change is good," Andy replied, stretching out his legs and crossing his ankles. "Especially with you by my side."

"Who would've thought?" Cassie chuckled, leaning back as the rocker moved with a comforting rhythm. "From stitching dresses to repairing fences, I never pictured this kind of life."

"Nor I," Andy confessed. "I imagined a ranch filled with cattle, not a partner who fills it with laughter and...well, love."

"Love," she echoed softly. The idea seemed as tangible as the fabric she worked with every day—a material she had learned to shape and mold into something cherished.

"Who knows what tomorrow holds?" Andy said, reaching over to take her hand. His touch was firm and reassuring. "But I think as long as we face it together, it'll be all right."

"Better than all right," Cassie corrected gently. She squeezed his hand in return, feeling the roughness of a rancher's calluses intertwine with the delicate precision of a seamstress's fingers. "I think we're going to do all we set out to do and more."

"Right again," he said with a grin.

Cassie leaned her head against Andy's shoulder, content in the day of work she'd put in and their future together.

Chapter Six

Cassie's knife danced along the cutting board, her hands sure and deft as she sliced through carrots and celery. The kitchen was alive with the scents of simmering broth and fresh vegetables. Andy stood opposite her, his dark head bowed over a pot as he stirred the contents with a wooden spoon, a small furrow of concentration etched between his brows.

"Smells heavenly," Cassie remarked, pushing a strand of blond hair from her forehead with the back of her hand. "Soup's always been a favorite of mine on chilly evenings."

Andy glanced up, his eyes crinkling at the corners as he smiled. "Mine too. Learned to make do with what we had in the orphanage. Soup can be a feast or a simple meal, depending on what's at hand."

Cassie paused, the last slice of carrot falling silently onto the pile. "You've never mentioned much about your past before. What was it like for you? My foundling home felt like a real home because of the love Mrs. Jackson poured into us."

Setting down the spoon, Andy leaned against the counter, his gaze distant but not darkened by the memories. "It was a life full of uncertainties. Never knew where the next meal would come from, or if there'd be enough to go around. But it taught me to be resourceful, to appreciate what I have."

"Resourcefulness seems to be a trait you carried into ranching," Cassie observed, empathy warming her voice.

"Sure did," he agreed with a nod. "Took every bit of grit I had to start up the ranch. It's a hard life, but I reckon it's worth it." Andy's hands faltered, the spoon hovering above the pot as if caught in a momentary lapse. "My folks passed when I was little," he began, his voice softer now, tinged with the weight of bygone years. "The orphanage was no nurturing homestead, that's for sure. But it was either get tough or get trampled."

Cassie set her knife aside, wiping her hands on her apron as she turned to face him fully, her interest etched in every line of her attentive posture. "And yet here you are, carving out a life," she said, the admiration clear in her tone.

Andy chuckled, though the sound held little mirth. "I think if I can tame this land, make something of my own, then all that struggle...it'd mean something." He shook his head. "I always knew I wanted to be a rancher. The orphanage...it was here in Texas, and I knew who I wanted to be. I think it was good for me. If I had parents who raised me, who knows where I would be now."

"The two of us...both orphans...were raised so differently. I like to think we can take over the world one small piece at a time."

There was a pause as their eyes met across the steam rising from the pot, and for a heartbeat, time seemed to stand still in the small kitchen. Then, as if roused by some unspoken agreement, Cassie turned back to her task.

"Let me show you how to really bring out the flavors in these veggies," Cassie said, her voice light, as she took the lead at the stove. She reached for the herbs growing on the windowsill, crumbling them between deft fingers. The scent of basil and thyme soon mingled with the richness of the broth.

"Smells like heaven, Cassie," Andy remarked, watching her movements with an appreciation that went beyond the culinary skills she displayed.

"Wait till you taste it," she teased, a playful edge to her words as she expertly sautéed the onions until they were translucent and golden.

The room filled with the mouthwatering aroma of garlic and butter as the vegetables sizzled in the pan.

"Never seen anyone handle a skillet quite like you," Andy said, his gaze lingering on her with an affection that was no longer just about the food.

She added just a pinch of salt, and his mouth started watering at the smell.

"Goodness, Cassie," Andy said, a smile playing on his lips. "You've got a real knack for this."

Her cheeks flushed with pleasure at the compliment. "Thank you, Andy. Cooking's always been a bit like magic to me."

He watched her taste the broth, her eyes closing briefly in satisfaction. He felt a warmth spreading through his chest, an affection that simmered like the stew, quiet yet undeniable.

"It's definitely magic," he murmured, more to himself than to her.

The conversation shifted as Cassie set down the wooden spoon and wiped her hands on her apron. "I've been working on a new dress design," she began, a spark of excitement in her eyes. She sketched an outline in the air with her fingers. "Something elegant, yet functional for life out here."

"Functional and frills don't often mix on a ranch," Andy quipped, though he admired her creative spirit.

Cassie's brows knit together slightly. "Maybe so, but a woman likes to feel pretty, even when she's miles from the nearest town."

"True enough," he conceded, "but it's got to stand up to the work too." His voice was gentle, not wanting to quash her enthusiasm.

"Perhaps a compromise then?" she suggested, her tone hopeful. "Sturdy fabric for the skirts, but with some special touches on the bodice or sleeves?"

"Sounds fair," Andy agreed with a nod. "A bit of beauty woven into the day's toil can't hurt."

"Exactly!" Cassie beamed, pleased with their common ground. "I'll make something that turns heads and holds up to a hard day's work."

"Can't wait to see it," he said, his admiration for her resourcefulness growing by the minute. As they found harmony in their differing views, Andy realized that life on the ranch might just be brighter with Cassie's touch—and her beside him.

CASSIE THUMBED THROUGH the pages of her sketchbook, her gaze flitting between the rough designs and Andy's expectant face. "How about this one?" she asked, pointing to a drawing. "A split riding skirt, perhaps? Practical for everyday ranch work, but with a bit of flair when you hitch it up."

"Split skirt, huh?" Andy scratched his chin thoughtfully. "Sounds like it could work. Easy to move in, I would think. Preserves a woman's modesty as she's riding and working on the ranch."

"Exactly," Cassie agreed, her eyes brightening. "And I can add some subtle embroidery along the hem—just enough to catch the eye without being too...froofy."

He chuckled at her choice of words. "Froofy. That's a new one. But sure, sounds like it'd hold up better than full skirts if you're hopping on and off a horse."

"Then it's settled." Cassie closed her sketchbook with a soft thump, satisfaction etched across her features. "Practicality meets prettiness."

"Best of both worlds," Andy nodded, impressed by how easily they were navigating this uncharted territory together. "You've got quite the knack for this, Cassie."

"Thanks, Andy. It means a lot, especially coming from you." She glanced down at her apron, smudged with flour, yet somehow it now felt like a badge of honor.

"Compromise," he mused aloud, "it's not so bad when you've got the right partner."

"Agreed," she said with a smile. "It's all about give and take."

"Looks like we're getting pretty good at that," Andy observed, warmth spreading through him as he watched her tuck a loose strand of blond hair behind her ear. "And who knows? Maybe your designs will start a new trend out here on the prairie."

"Wouldn't that be something?" Cassie laughed, already picturing the women of the town twirling in her creations. "I'll make sure you get credit as my muse."

"Me, a muse?" He feigned a look of disbelief. "Now I've heard everything."

"For someone who didn't want any 'froof,' you're full of surprises, Mr. Forsythe," she teased, her blue eyes sparkling with mirth.

"Only the best for my wife," he replied.

ANDY REACHED FOR THE hem of the dress pattern, holding it up against Cassie's frame as she stood still, arms slightly raised. "You know, it might just work," he admitted with a hint of admiration in his voice.

Cassie met his gaze, her lips curving into a gentle smile. "With some modifications, but yes, I think we're onto something." She lowered her arms and stepped closer, her hands finding their way to the fabric still clasped in his. Together, they folded the pattern, their fingers brushing lightly.

"Thank you, Andy," she said softly. Her appreciation was not just for the compromise over the dress but for the ease with which they were learning to navigate their partnership.

"Anything for you, Cassie," Andy replied, sincerity shining in his dark eyes. He released the pattern and instead wrapped his arms around her waist, drawing her into an affectionate embrace. It was a simple gesture, yet it held the promise of unspoken depth between them.

She rested her head against his chest, listening to the steady rhythm of his heart. A shared laugh bubbled up from within her as she thought about how far they had come, from practical strangers to partners in every sense of the word. "We do make quite the team, don't we?"

"We do," Andy chuckled, his breath warm against her hair. "I never imagined that I'd be helping design dresses. People are going to be talking about us for a long time to come."

"Only the best kind of talk, I hope," Cassie teased, tilting her head back to look at him.

"Of course." He tapped her nose playfully.

"Imagine all the dreams we could chase," Cassie mused, her blue eyes alight with the thoughts of dresses designed and a ranch flourishing.

"Let's chase them all," Andy whispered, his ambition for success now intertwined with her creative aspirations. They both knew there would be hurdles, but the foundation they were building was solid, grounded in mutual respect and burgeoning love.

Chapter Seven

Cassie and Andy settled by the river with their picnic spread. A quilt was draped over the grass, a few sandwiches neatly wrapped in cloth, and a jug of sweet iced tea sat between them.

"Can't remember the last time I had a day this fine," Cassie said, her blue eyes sparkling with contentment as she took a bite of her sandwich.

"Out here, it's like the rest of the world doesn't exist," Andy replied, a smile playing on his lips. His dark eyes reflected the shimmering water, and he seemed to savor the moment just as much as the food.

They exchanged stories of childhood antics and dreams, laughter mingling with the gentle burble of the river. Cassie told of her days teaching, her voice tinged with a dry humor that made Andy chuckle.

"Children can be quite the handful," she said, shaking her head at the memory. "I do not miss those days."

"Maybe you prefer cattle to children?" Andy quipped, raising an eyebrow playfully. "At least they don't ask for homework help."

"Or scream when they don't get their way," Cassie added, and they both laughed.

After the meal, they wandered along the riverbank, hand in hand, comforted by each other's presence. The afternoon sun warmed their backs, and the soft rustle of leaves in the breeze accompanied their steps.

"Careful there," Andy warned as Cassie navigated around a cluster of rocks, but just as she nodded, her foot caught on a loose stone. With a gasp, she stumbled forward, but Andy's reflexes were quick. He reached out, wrapping a firm arm around her waist, steadying her before she could fall.

"Got you," he murmured, his breath close to her ear.

For a fleeting second, their eyes locked—a storm of emotions swirling in the depths of Andy's gaze. Cassie's heart skipped a beat, her breath caught in the sudden intensity between them. She noticed how his grip was both protective and gentle, and something within her stirred.

She stood on tiptoe and pressed her lips to his. Andy's heart raced as Cassie's soft lips met his, a rush of emotions surging through him. The kiss was tender yet full of unspoken promises, a silent confession of the growing affection they held for each other. They lingered there by the river, their embrace deepening as the world faded away around them.

When they finally parted, a warmth lingered between them, filling the space with an unspoken understanding. Andy's gaze locked with Cassie's, his dark eyes reflecting the glint of newfound love.

Cassie's cheeks flushed a delicate pink, her blue eyes meeting his with a mix of vulnerability and courage. They'd kissed many times, but usually under the cover of night, in their bed. This kiss...it was one she'd wanted for a long while. A kiss that didn't have to lead into something else. A kiss just for the sake of kissing.

"Thank you," she whispered, her voice barely above the sound of the flowing river. It was all she could manage, lost in the unspoken words that danced between them.

"If that's my reward for saving you from falling, I may have to help you fall a bit..."

Cassie and Andy walked through a break in the trees. Before them, the land opened up to a sea of wildflowers, swaying gently under the touch of a playful breeze. Cassie's eyes shone like the clear blue sky above, reflecting her unspoken affection for the vibrant canvas spread at their feet.

"Look at this," she breathed out, stepping into the field with care, as if each flower were a precious gem.

Andy watched her, the corners of his mouth turning up. He'd never seen her quite so taken by something simple before. With a quick scan of the colorful blooms, he leaned down and began picking a selection, his fingers choosing with an innate sense of what would please her.

"Here," he said, extending the bouquet toward Cassie. His smile was shy.

"For me?" Cassie's formal tone softened, touched by the sincerity in his simple gift. "They're beautiful, Andy. Thank you." She accepted the flowers, and her heart felt lighter.

"Thought they'd brighten up the place," Andy replied, his voice casual but his dark eyes betraying the depth of his sentiment.

"They will," Cassie agreed, tucking a stray blond strand of hair behind her ear, her thoughts already turning to how the flowers would look in a vase on the dining room table.

In the kitchen, apron tied neatly around her waist, Cassie set about preparing dinner. The aroma of herbs and spices filled the space, a savory invitation to relax and savor life's simple pleasures. They moved in an effortless dance around each other, Andy chopping vegetables as Cassie stirred the pot on the stove.

"Hand me the salt, would you?" Cassie asked, glancing over her shoulder with a playful smirk.

"Sure thing," Andy responded, passing the salt shaker, his hand briefly brushing hers. A current of warmth passed between them, sparking a shared moment of amusement.

"Careful now," he teased, "wouldn't want the food to end up too seasoned."

"Wouldn't dream of it," she said.

"Smells like heaven, Cassie," Andy complimented, his gaze lingering on her just a moment longer than necessary.

"Wait until you taste it," she replied, confident in her culinary skills and the evening that lay ahead, full of promise and the tender stirrings of love.

Cassie reached for the bag of flour, her fingers still slick from the butter she'd been using to grease the pie pan. The white powder slipped through her grasp, a cloud of flour billowing out and settling over her dress like fresh snow on a winter's morning.

"Land sakes," she muttered, her cheeks turning the color of the ripe tomatoes sitting on the counter.

Andy couldn't help but chuckle at the sight, his deep laugh echoing warmly in the kitchen. "Here, let me," he said, stepping closer with a damp cloth in hand. His fingers brushed hers as he gently wiped at the floury mess, sending a jolt through them both.

"Thank you, Andy," Cassie said, her voice a soft murmur, feeling a flutter in her belly at his proximity.

"Anytime, Cassie," he replied, his eyes not quite meeting hers.

With the minor disaster averted, they sat at the modest wooden table, plates piled high with the fruits of their labor. The room was filled with the rich aroma of roasted chicken and the tangy sweetness of apple pie, which awaited them for dessert.

"This is delicious," Cassie praised, taking a bite of the vegetables that Andy had so carefully prepared. "You've got a real talent for cooking."

Andy's face bloomed with a bashful pride. "Well, I do my best," he said. "But it's your company that makes it taste better."

Cassie took Andy's hand and led him out into the cool embrace of the evening. Their footsteps crunched softly against the gravel path as they strolled beneath a sky scattered with stars, each one a distant firefly winking down at them from eternity.

"Isn't it a beautiful night?" she remarked.

"Every night's beautiful with you by my side," Andy murmured, his words carrying the weight of the truth he felt within.

As the pair approached a small pond, they found an old wooden bench patiently awaiting their company. Cassie seated herself, smoothing the fabric of her dress, while Andy joined her.

"Look at the stars reflecting on the water," Cassie said softly.

"Like diamonds spilled across black velvet," Andy said.

Cassie leaned her head against Andy's shoulder, finding comfort in the solid feel of him beside her.

"You're something else, you know that?" Andy's voice broke through the silence.

She turned to look at him, her heart skipping a beat. "Oh? And what's that supposed to mean?"

"Your strength, Cassie," he said, his dark eyes earnest in the moonlight. "The way you handle life with such determination. It's admirable."

"Well, I've had to be strong," she admitted, tucking a stray blond curl behind her ear. "Dreams don't just happen. They need someone to chase them."

Cassie and Andy made their way back to the house.

"Look at that sky," Cassie murmured, her voice a whisper in the vastness around them.

Andy glanced upward, then followed her gaze just as a streak of light carved across the night. "Make a wish," he said softly, his dark eyes reflecting the stars.

Cassie closed her eyes. She wished silently, fervently, for a life brimming with happiness alongside the man beside her.

"May it come true," Andy whispered as if he knew her silent plea.

Andy reached out, his fingers intertwining with hers, the contact sending warmth up her arm. He leaned in, his lips brushing her cheek in a tender kiss that stirred something deep within her. It was an affirmation, a silent acknowledgment of the bond they were forging.

"Come on," Andy said, his voice low, laced with a gentle urgency that made her pulse quicken. He led her toward the house, their hands clasped, a current of anticipation guiding their steps.

In the seclusion of their home, the simple act of closing the door marked the start of something new. They stood there, hearts beating in rhythm, as Andy turned to face her. The distance between them vanished, replaced by a closeness that felt as natural as drawing breath.

In the softness of the sheets, beneath the sheltering roof of their burgeoning life together, they surrendered to the love that had been quietly growing between them.

Afterward, Cassie nestled into the softness of the quilt, her eyes tracing the moonlit patterns on the wall. The day's laughter still echoed in her heart. She turned to her side, facing Andy, his steady breathing a soothing rhythm in the quiet room.

"Today was something special, wasn't it?" she whispered, her voice barely louder than the rustle of the sheets.

"Sure was," Andy replied, his smile audible in the darkness. "I think days like this are what life's all about."

"Seems like it," Cassie agreed.

Andy reached out, his hand finding hers under the covers. Their fingers entwined, as natural as the intertwining roots of an old oak tree. He leaned closer, his breath warm against her cheek.

"I'm looking forward to building something with you, Cassie. Not just the ranch, but...everything."

Cassie felt a shiver of joy, the kind that comes when the future is ripe with possibilities. She squeezed his hand, her answer clear in the pressure of her grip.

"Me too, Andy. Me too."

"Goodnight, Cassie," Andy murmured, his voice low and husky with emotion.

"Goodnight, Andy," she replied, her words floating on a sigh.

In the space between wakefulness and sleep, Cassie's mind wandered to images of a bustling dress shop, its windows filled with her creations, vibrant and alive. She saw Andy at the ranch, his face alight with pride as he surveyed fields of thriving crops and healthy cattle.

Her dreams were the same as his. A future together, filled with love and success. What more could they ask for?

Chapter Eight

Cassie watched the horse-drawn carriage grow closer, her heart drumming a rapid beat against her ribs. The visitor from Dallas had finally arrived, bringing with her the critical gaze of high society and the chance for Cassie to realize a dream she'd nursed alongside every stitch and hem.

It had only been six months since she'd arrived in Texas, and already it felt as if all of her dreams were coming true. If she could get this client, then possibly, she would be in a position to get more just like her.

The carriage creaked to a stop in front of the ranch house, where Cassie stood smoothing the fabric of her apron. A woman stepped out, her dress finer than any Cassie had ever laid eyes on, with layers of silk that whispered secrets of wealth and status. She introduced herself as Mrs. Montgomery.

"Mrs. Forsythe, I've come quite a ways," Mrs. Montgomery said, eyeing the humble surroundings before her gaze landed on Cassie's portfolio of designs laid out on the porch table.

"Please, call me Cassie," she replied, with a polite nod, guiding the woman to her work.

As Mrs. Montgomery perusing the sketches, her lips pursed in an expression that could curdle milk. Cassie felt the gnawing twist of worry in her belly. Would her work meet this critical eye? She tried to keep her tone light and hopeful. "I've got a variety of styles here. Each one is my own design."

"I see." Mrs. Montgomery's finger hovered over two drawings. "My daughter is getting married. I want something unique—a blend of these two designs."

"Absolutely," Cassie responded, her mind already racing through the logistics of combining the elegant bodice of one with the flowing skirt of the other. "I can do that."

"Can you?" Mrs. Montgomery challenged, her scrutinizing gaze not letting up. "It must be perfect. My daughter deserves nothing less."

Cassie nodded, her confidence a brittle shell that she prayed didn't crack. "It will be. Perfect, I mean."

They spent a moment discussing the price, and Cassie felt her heart jump into her throat when Mrs. Montgomery didn't quibble with the price she asked, which was double what she would normally charge.

"Very well. I expect nothing short of excellence." With those parting words, Mrs. Montgomery turned, leaving Cassie with the weight of expectation pressing down on her shoulders.

"Perfect," Cassie whispered to herself, watching the carriage roll away.

CASSIE THREADED HER needle with a fresh length of ivory silk. She heard the familiar creak of the porch as Andy stepped up from the dusty yard, his shadow briefly eclipsing the light.

"Evening, Cassie," he called out.

"Evening, Andy." She set her sewing aside, her fingers still tingling with the excitement and dread of her new commission. "You ever have one of those moments when you wonder if you've bitten off more than you can chew?"

Andy leaned against the door frame, a smile tugging at his lips. "Every time I look out at that herd wondering if they'll make it through winter. But you, Cassie, you're the best seamstress in the county. Mrs. Montgomery's daughter will be the envy of Dallas when she's wearing one of your creations."

His confidence was like a balm to her frayed nerves. "Thank you, Andy. I needed to hear that." She glanced up at him, noting the furrow between his brows, a telltale sign that his mind was turning over something serious.

"Speaking of biting off more than we can chew," he started, scratching at the stubble on his chin, "I've been saving for a good while now, and I'm at a bit of crossroads." He paused, considering his words. "I can either expand the ranch, buy some adjoining land I've had my eye on, or get some help around here, hire an extra hand. But I can't swing both, not with the way money's tight."

Cassie pondered his dilemma, her own worries momentarily set aside. "That's a tough choice, Andy. But whatever you decide, it'll be the right call. You've got a head for these things."

"Maybe so," he replied, his dark eyes reflecting a mix of hope and caution. "But it sure would be easier if I could just do both, wouldn't it?"

"Wouldn't we all like that," she said with a chuckle, picking up her needlework again. "But we make do, don't we? And we make it work."

"We do," Andy agreed, stepping into the house to wash up for supper, leaving Cassie to her stitches and thoughts, the last rays of sunlight winking out behind the horizon.

Cassie set her needlework aside, folding it carefully before placing it in her sewing basket. She rose from the chair on the porch, her skirts rustling softly as she stepped through the doorway into the cozy warmth of the kitchen where Andy was washing his hands at the basin.

"Andy," she said, "I've been doing some thinking."

He turned, drying his hands on a cloth, a questioning look in his dark eyes. "Oh? What's on your mind?"

"I've got some money saved up," Cassie said, tucking a loose strand of hair behind her ear. "From my teaching days back East. It's not a fortune, but...do you think it could help with your decision? About the land or hiring help?"

Andy stopped mid-wipe, his brow creasing. "You'd do that?" he asked, a note of hesitation in his voice. "Put your hard-earned savings into this ranch?"

She walked over to him, her eyes earnest. "Of course, I would. I spend your money on groceries and whatever else without a second thought. It's only right. We're partners in this, aren't we?"

Andy looked down at the worn wooden floorboards, his jaw working slightly. He met her gaze again, his features softening. "You make a fair point, Cassie. But it's your money. You worked for it."

"Which makes it our money," she interjected gently, reaching out to touch his arm. "Think about it, won't you?"

A smile tugged at the corner of his mouth, and he nodded, placing his hand over hers. "All right, I'll think on it. You sure have a way of making sense when I need it most."

She gave his arm a reassuring squeeze, the corners of her mouth lifting into an affectionate smile. "That's what I'm here for."

CASSIE'S FINGERS TREMBLED slightly as she placed the final stitch on the dress, the delicate fabric whispering under her touch. She held it up to the light, inspecting every seam with a critical eye. It was her finest work yet - a harmonious blend of two of her most admired designs, destined for a wedding in Dallas. A proud smile tugged at her lips.

"Ready?" Andy leaned against the doorway, his dark eyes taking in the sight of the dress.

"Ready," Cassie affirmed, folding the garment carefully into a box lined with tissue.

Together, they boarded the train from Fort Worth to Dallas. As buildings and bustling streets replaced open fields, Cassie clutched the box closer.

"Stop worrying," Andy nudged her gently. "Your dress is perfect. And it will be worn by the bride at some fancy wedding. Soon, there will be a herd of women trying to knock our door down to get more of your dresses."

The wealthy woman from Dallas was all polished elegance, her scrutinizing gaze sweeping over Cassie's offering. Relief bloomed when her stern expression melted into delight.

"Exquisite!" The woman exclaimed, tracing the lace with a gloved finger. "My daughter will be the belle of her wedding."

Her friends, equally impressed, clustered around, murmurs of admiration filling the room. Before Cassie could catch her breath, orders for three more dresses were placed, each with a tight deadline that made her heart race.

"Can you manage it?" Andy asked quietly as they left, the weight of the task settling on her shoulders.

"I have to," she replied, determination in her voice.

On the return journey, Andy's voice broke the comfortable silence.

"About your offer..." He cleared his throat, the setting sun casting shadows across his strong features. "I'll take some of that money you saved. We'll expand the land and hire a hand."

Cassie's weariness from the day's excitement was swept away by the rush of gratitude and love she felt for this man who stood by her side.

"Thank you, Andy," Cassie said, her voice soft but full of emotion. "That means the world to me."

"Don't thank me. You're the one helping me out," he said simply, reaching out to squeeze her hand.

CASSIE SAT HUNCHED over her sewing machine, the hum of its needle a constant companion as daylight waned into dusk. Bolts of fabric sprawled across the worktable like wildflowers in a prairie, their colors vibrant under the lamplight. Her fingers worked deftly, piecing together seams with the precision that had become her signature.

"Supper's on the table," Andy called from the kitchen, his voice pulling her from the trance of her craft.

"Already?" Cassie glanced at the window, surprised to see the sky painted in twilight hues. She hadn't even noticed the passage of time.

"Yep. Made your favorite - stew." He appeared in the doorway, an apron tied around his waist, a smile softening the rugged lines of his face.

"Thank you," she said, standing to stretch her cramped limbs. "I didn't realize how late it got."

"That's because you start work before the sun comes up and barely take time to swallow a meal before you're at it again," he teased, leading her to the table where a steaming pot awaited.

Cassie chuckled, but guilt gnawed at her as they sat down. In the past few days, while her focus was riveted on fulfilling dress orders, cooking had fallen by the wayside, and Andy had stepped in without complaint.

"Feels strange, not having had a hand in dinner," she admitted, poking at the carrots in her bowl.

"Strange in a good way, I hope." Andy raised his eyebrows, passing her the cornbread.

"Maybe for you," Cassie sighed, taking a bite of the bread, its warmth comforting. "I feel like a terrible wife, leaving all this to you."

"Hey now," he reached across the table, covering her hand with his. "You're doing what needs to be done. We're a team, remember? I can handle pots and pans for a spell."

She squeezed his hand, grateful for his understanding. "Just a few more days. Once these dresses are delivered, things will get back to normal."

"Take the time you need, Cassie. Your work's as important as anything I might have to do," Andy reassured her, his dark eyes earnest.

"Thanks," she smiled, the weight in her chest lifting a little. "But I'm making you a feast to make up for it. As soon as these stitches are set and the last hem is sewn."

"Looking forward to it," he winked.

As they finished their meal, talking about everything and nothing, Cassie felt the love and companionship that made every hardship worthwhile.

She reached out and took his hand. "Most men wouldn't put up with the hours I'm working, and I appreciate that you think my dream is as important as yours."

He brought her fingers to his lips. "I never could understand why a man would think what he did was more important than what his wife did." He shook his head. "I'm just thankful for the extra income that's making my life easier."

CASSIE HOISTED THE satchel containing her meticulously crafted dresses onto the carriage seat, the leather creaking under the weight. Deborah climbed up beside her, tucking a stray wisp of hair behind her ear, her gaze lingering on the parcel with quiet admiration.

"Can't believe you're pulling all this off, Cassie," Deborah murmured, as the horses began their steady trot toward the train station in Fort Worth.

Cassie's hands rested on the reins, her knuckles white against the worn leather. "Truth be told, it's been a bit harder than I thought it would be," she confessed, her eyes fixed on the road ahead. "Between the sewing and keeping house, I'm stretched thinner than morning mist."

Deborah glanced at her sister, noting the faint shadows beneath Cassie's blue eyes. "You know, Jane's got a knack for cooking and wouldn't mind some extra money. Maybe she could help with the evening meals and tidying up?"

Cassie's brow furrowed at the thought, the idea swirling like a new pattern in her mind. "Hire Jane?" she echoed, pondering. "Wouldn't be too proud to admit I need the help, but..."

"Sometimes, pride's has to take a back seat to practicality," Deborah cut in softly. "She'd be glad for the work, and you'd have more time for your dressmaking."

A smile tugged at the corner of Cassie's lips. "Might just take you up on that suggestion, Deb," she said, a newfound lightness to her voice as they continued down the dusty road toward opportunity.

CASSIE AND DEBORAH stepped out of the train, their arms laden with carefully wrapped packages. Cassie's heart fluttered like the hem of a petticoat caught in a breeze—today was the day her creations would face judgment.

"Here we are," Cassie said, squaring her shoulders as they approached the grand house that had placed the order.

"Your dressmaking's about to be the talk of the town," Deborah added with an encouraging smile.

Cassie hoped so. With each knock on the polished oak door, her confidence stitched itself firmer. The door swung open, revealing the eager faces of the Dallas elite gathered inside. Compliments flowed freely as Cassie unveiled the dresses. Relief softened her posture. They were smitten.

"Could you combine this lace with that bodice for my niece's birthday party?" one lady asked, pointing to two different gowns.

"Absolutely," Cassie replied, her head buzzing with new designs.

Cassie was glad she'd thought to bring her sketchbook. She watched as two women pored over the pages.

By the time they left, orders were penciled into Cassie's book, each one a promise of growth for her business. Yet, as they were on the train to return to Fort Worth, a knot of worry formed in her gut. Hiring Jane meant discussing money with Andy—an undertaking more daunting than any dress she'd fashioned.

That night, after a supper of stewed chicken and fresh biscuits, Cassie lingered at the table, sipping her tea as Andy cleaned the plates. She watched his back, the way his muscles moved beneath his shirt—a dance of strength and purpose.

"Deborah had an idea today," Cassie began, her voice trailing like a leaf on a stream.

Andy turned, wiping his hands on a cloth. "Oh? What might that be?"

"About hiring Jane to help around here. With the cooking and cleaning, just for a couple hours each day." Cassie folded her hands in her lap, awaiting his response.

Andy leaned against the counter, considering. "Makes sense to me," he said after a pause. "You've got your hands full with those dresses."

"Really?" Cassie blinked, surprised by his easy agreement.

"Sure," Andy chuckled. "I think I'd like to taste something other than my own cooking for a change."

Relief washed over Cassie like a gentle rain. She smiled, warmth spreading through her chest. "Thank you, Andy. It means the world."

"Anything for you, Cassie." His eyes met hers, steady and sincere. "We're in this together."

Cassie was thrilled. She hadn't talked to Jane yet, but she was certain her sister would agree. It would be so much better than trying to do it all herself.

Chapter Nine

Cassie walked down the path to Susan's house right after breakfast the following morning. The air was crisp, and she wrapped her shawl tighter around her shoulders. Today, she was on a mission to secure Jane's help so she could put more of her time and energy into her burgeoning dressmaking business.

Susan greeted Cassie warmly at the door, her blond hair catching the sunlight. "Morning, Cassie. Come on in," she said, stepping aside to let her enter.

"Thank you, Susan. I won't take but a minute of your time," Cassie replied, stepping into the cozy kitchen where the smell of freshly baked bread filled the air.

Jane was there, her youthful face brightening as Cassie entered. "Good morning, Cassie!" she chirped, setting down the dishcloth she was holding.

"Morning, Jane. I have a proposition for you," Cassie said, getting straight to the point. "I need help. Cooking, cleaning, and maybe learning a bit about sewing. Would you be interested?"

Jane's eyes sparkled with excitement. "Oh, yes! That would be wonderful!"

"Good," Cassie nodded, pleased. "We can agree on a fair salary, and you'll keep staying here with Susan, as I don't have the space."

"Of course, Cassie. Thank you," Jane beamed, nodding in agreement. Jane had been the last of the ten orphans to travel to Texas and had been staying with Susan since her arrival.

Later that afternoon, Jane arrived at Cassie's, apron tied neatly around her waist. She quickly set to work, tidying up the place with an efficiency that impressed Cassie. While pots clattered and the broom swished across the wooden floor, Cassie sat at her worktable, cutting patterns from brown paper.

"Cassie, where should I put these scraps?" Jane asked, holding a handful of fabric remnants.

"Over there, in the basket by the window," Cassie directed without looking up.

"All right, Cassie," Jane said. Jane had known Cassie her entire life, but it was different to be employed by her.

Jane cooked them a simple yet savory meal, and they had a quiet lunch together.

Cassie was thrilled by the time Jane was freeing up for her, and she was glad that Jane seemed happy to do the work.

CASSIE WATCHED AS JANE bustled around the kitchen, her apron swishing with each brisk step. The aroma of stewing beef and fresh bread filled the air, a testament to Jane's growing culinary skills.

"John Miller was asking about me at the general store," Jane mentioned casually, stacking plates with a clink. "And George Smith said he'd fix that wobbly shelf if I baked him one of those apple pies like the one I made last week."

Cassie chuckled, shaking her head while threading her needle with practiced ease. "Jane, you've got the whole town's batch of bachelors on a string. Might be time to pick one and let the others down easy."

With a playful toss of her chestnut hair, Jane laughed, the sound bright and unburdened. "Oh, Cassie, but it's so much fun being courted! Besides, how can I choose just one?"

The door creaked open and Andy stepped in, his dark hair tousled from the day's work. Behind him, a tall figure loomed, wiping dusty hands on rough denim.

"Evening, ladies," Andy greeted them. "This here's Robert Myers, my new hired hand."

"Please, call me Bob," said the newcomer, his voice gruff but polite.

"Nice to meet you, Bob," Cassie replied with a nod, her gaze flickering between him and Jane.

Dinner passed with a curious undercurrent, the air charged with an energy that wasn't entirely amicable. Cassie noted the way Jane's brow furrowed ever so slightly when Bob spoke, and how his responses to her chatter were terse, almost dismissive.

"Pass the salt, please," Jane requested, her tone holding a hint of ice that hadn't been there before.

"Sure," Bob replied, sliding the shaker across the table without meeting her eyes.

Later, as they cleared the dishes, Cassie leaned close to Andy. "What do you make of those two? They're like oil and water."

Andy's mouth twitched into a knowing smile. "Sometimes, that's just how it starts. Give it time."

The last of the supper plates were put back into the cabinet, and Cassie watched as Bob offered a curt nod to Jane. "Suppose I should walk you back," he mumbled, avoiding her gaze.

"Suppose you should," Jane responded, her voice edged with a playfulness that didn't quite reach her eyes.

Cassie shook her head slightly as she threaded a needle, her fingers nimbly catching the cotton. The soft whisper of fabric against her skin was comforting as she focused on the dress pattern spread across the table.

"Those two are like a summer storm brewing," Andy remarked from where he lounged against the doorframe, his arms crossed over his chest.

"Could be. Or maybe just a drizzle that'll pass," Cassie said, glancing up at him with a small smile.

"Speaking of weather, you should've seen Bob today trying to mend the fence by the creek," Andy chuckled. "He swore he could handle the mule, but that beast dragged him a good ten yards before he let go of the rope."

"Is he all right?" Cassie asked, amusement dancing in her blue eyes.

"Nothing wounded but his pride," Andy said, the laughter in his voice echoing in the cozy kitchen.

"Good help is hard to find," Cassie mused, returning her attention to the dress. She pressed her lips together, then spoke up again. "Andy, I've been thinking. Maybe it's time we stop offering delivery for the dresses to Dallas."

"You think?" Andy leaned in closer, his interest piqued.

"I do. If they want one of my dresses, they can come here. It's putting too much strain on me and not adding much to our earnings."

"Sounds sensible," Andy agreed with a firm nod. "You shouldn't have to run yourself ragged."

"Exactly." Cassie smiled, feeling the warmth of his support. "I'm heading out to my shop for a little while. I need to use my sewing machine for this next part."

Hours later, Cassie set down her needle and thread, rubbing the fatigue from her eyes. She glanced around the cozy confines of her dress shop, where rolls of fabric lay stacked in haphazard towers. With a thoughtful frown, she turned to Andy, who was leaning against the doorframe, his arms crossed over his chest as he watched her work.

"Andy, this place is getting crowded," Cassie began, gesturing toward the overflowing shelves. "I need more space to display the fabrics—new shelves would do wonders."

Andy pushed away from the doorframe and walked over, carefully examining the clutter. "You're right," he said, running a hand through his hair. "More shelves could line that wall there. Would make it easier for your customers to see everything you've got."

"Exactly," Cassie nodded with determination, her blond hair catching the light from the lantern. "And while we're at it, I'm thinking of striking a bargain with the general store. Special deals on fabric could help both our businesses."

"Smart thinking," Andy agreed, a glint of admiration in his gaze. "Your head's always full of plans, Cassie. It's one of the many things I admire about you."

She offered him a grateful smile before a new thought struck her. "I can't keep up with custom orders alone anymore. If only I had time to sew some dresses ahead of time—ready-made ones to sell right off the shelf."

"Have you considered that?" Andy asked, tilting his head to one side. "It might draw in more ladies, looking for something quick and fashionable."

"Of course, I have," Cassie replied with a touch of pride. "As soon as I find the time, I'll stitch up a bunch of dresses. Give the women of this town a taste of convenience and style."

"Sounds like a plan," Andy chuckled. "Just remember, don't work yourself too thin."

"Thank you, Andy," Cassie said warmly. "With your help, it seems there's nothing we can't do." She picked up her sewing once more, but now with a renewed sense of purpose, envisioning a future where her dreams were neatly folded and displayed on brand-new shelves, ready for the world to embrace.

CASSIE AND ANDY PREPARED for bed. "You need more rest," Andy said gently, brushing a stray lock of hair from Cassie's forehead.

"I know," she sighed, her resolve softening in the candlelight. "I'll try to sleep more."

In the quiet sanctuary of their room, they came together with a tenderness that spoke more than words ever could. The world outside faded away as they reaffirmed their love, drawing comfort from each other's presence.

Afterward, as Andy's steady breathing signaled his journey into dreams, Cassie lay awake, tracing the familiar patterns on the ceiling. She thought about the bolts of fabric waiting to be transformed, the shelves that would soon hold her creations, and the ready-made dresses that would bring convenience to the busy lives of the women in town.

A spark of inspiration ignited within her, and she envisioned the perfect way to showcase her talents—a special dress for herself, one that would stand out at Sunday church. She imagined the gasps of admiration, the inquiries about where such a dress could be found, and she'd reply with a knowing smile, "Why, I make dresses like this for my shop."

She pictured the dress in her mind, elegant yet practical, a testament to her craft. Her current wardrobe, worn and functional, was no longer a reflection of the woman she was becoming. A new dress, created by her own hands, would invite others to share in the beauty she could offer.

Cassie slipped from the warmth of their bed, careful not to disturb Andy's slumber. The moonlight bathed the room in a soft glow, casting long shadows across the wooden floorboards. She tiptoed out to her shop, where scraps of fabric and unfinished projects lay in silent anticipation of her touch.

The hum of the sewing machine was a lullaby that failed to reach Andy's ears. Cassie lost herself in the rhythm of the needle, a new dress taking shape under her hands.

In the quiet hours of the night, as the clock ticked on, Andy stirred. He reached out for Cassie, expecting the familiar comfort of her presence. His hand met only cool sheets, and he opened his eyes to find her side of the bed empty. A frown tugged at his lips.

"Cassie?" he called softly, already knowing she wouldn't answer. He pushed himself out of bed, following the light he could see through one of the windows.

Andy found her there in her shop, surrounded by her creations, a look of fierce determination etched into her brow. He leaned against the doorway, watching her work with an ache in his heart. The silence between them was heavy with unspoken words.

"Can't sleep?" he asked.

Cassie jumped slightly, then flashed him a quick smile. "Just had an idea I couldn't ignore," she replied, her fingers never pausing in their dance.

"You need rest, Cassie. We both do."

"I will, soon. Just...let me finish this hem."

Andy nodded, though disappointment clouded his dark eyes. "I'll be waiting," he said, retreating back to their bed.

As he lay down again, listening to the distant whir of the sewing machine, Andy's thoughts wandered. He pondered the threads of ambition that wove through Cassie's spirit, admiring and yet fearing them. He loved her passion, her drive, but at moments like this, he couldn't shake the feeling that her business, her need to prove herself, was stealing her away from him.

Chapter Ten

Cassie's eyes snapped open as a wave of nausea surged through her. Clutching her stomach, she bolted from the bed and made a beeline for the kitchen basin. The coolness of the floorboards barely registered against her feet as another wave hit, and she found herself hunched over basin, retching.

"Cassie?" Andy's voice was groggy with sleep, but alert with concern. He shuffled in, rubbing his dark hair into further disarray, his eyes squinting against the early morning light seeping through the curtains.

"Are you all right?" he asked, standing beside her and placing a tentative hand on her back.

Cassie spat out the last of the bitter taste before she leaned back, resting against the wall. She met Andy's worried gaze with a hesitant one of her own.

"Andy...I think—I might be..." Her words trailed off as she nibbled her lip, summoning the courage to voice her suspicion.

"Be what?" he urged gently, his hand moving in slow circles on her back, trying to soothe her.

"Expecting," she whispered finally, the word feeling foreign yet heavy with implications.

"Expecting?" Andy repeated, his brain still foggy from sleep. "You mean—"

"A baby, yes." Cassie's voice was a mix of wonder and uncertainty. She watched as a myriad of emotions flickered across Andy's face—surprise, confusion, and something that looked like hope.

"Cassie, you must be mistaken," he said with a furrowed brow. "We both know that...well, I've always known children aren't possible for me."

"Maybe so, but my body feels different, Andy. I can't just ignore it," Cassie countered, her hands instinctively going to her abdomen as if to shield the secret it might be harboring.

"Perhaps it's something you ate," Andy suggested, trying to inject some practicality into the situation, though his voice betrayed a twinge of hope.

"Maybe," she conceded, but her intuition spoke louder than reason. "Brenda mentioned a midwife nearby, Mrs. Blakely. She'd know for sure."

"Then we'll have her set things straight. First thing, you go see this midwife," Andy decided, the words punctuating the silence that had fallen over them.

"Tomorrow," Cassie said. "I'll go first thing."

"Good," Andy replied, the corners of his mouth lifting slightly, offering a silent comfort amidst the uncertainty. "We'll figure this out."

Andy struggled to keep his focus as the cattle ambled around the dusty corral, their hooves kicking up small clouds that mirrored his scattered thoughts. Each moo seemed to echo with a question mark, reverberating with the soft possibility of "what if?"

"Confound it," he muttered under his breath when the calf he'd been trying to herd darted off in the wrong direction once more. He wasn't usually one to let his mind wander from the task at hand, but today, the fences and fields held no claim over his attention.

"Thinking about Cassie?" Bob, his ranch hand and friend, called out from atop the fence with a knowing grin. Andy nodded, the corners of his eyes crinkling slightly as he thought about the morning's revelation. What if she really was expecting?

"I am," Andy admitted, leaning against the wooden post for a moment's respite. "She's seeing Hortense Blakely today."

"Ah." Bob's grin softened into a gentle smile. "That kind of visit."

"Yep." Andy pushed off the post, feeling a sudden surge of nervous energy. "We might be...expanding our family."

Bob's eyebrows shot up. "I didn't think you two wanted children."

"Neither did we," Andy replied, his voice tinged with a cautious optimism that felt foreign on his tongue.

CASSIE'S HEART RACED as she sat in the modest parlor of Hortense Blakely's home, her hands folded neatly in her lap. The air smelled of herbs, a comforting scent that did little to ease the fluttering in her stomach.

"Mrs. Forsythe," Hortense began, her tone professional yet not unkind. "I have completed my examination."

Cassie met the midwife's steady gaze, bracing herself for the verdict.

"Congratulations, my dear. You are with child."

The words struck Cassandra like a summer thunderclap — sudden and startling, yet somehow expected. Her serious disposition wavered as she felt a smile tugging at her lips despite the gravity of the situation.

"Thank you, Mrs. Blakely," Cassie managed to say, her voice a blend of gratitude and trepidation. She couldn't help but wonder how they would manage the ranch, her dress shop, and a new baby. But to her surprise, she was thrilled with the idea.

"Take care now, and come see me should you need anything," Hortense offered, her eyes softening at the sight of the young woman's mixed emotions.

"Of course," Cassie replied, rising from her chair. As she stepped out onto the porch, she allowed herself a moment to breathe in the vastness of the sky above. It seemed to whisper promises of change, challenge, and unexpected joy.

The dishes clinked softly as Cassie cleared the table, her mind a whirlwind of thoughts and emotions. She could feel Andy's gaze on her, patient yet expectant. The evening sun cast a warm glow through the window, wrapping the kitchen in gold and amber. It was time.

"Andy," she said, "I went to see Hortense today."

She watched him pause, his hands stilling on the dish towel. His dark eyes locked onto hers, searching for the message behind her words.

"And?" he prompted when she hesitated a beat too long.

"I'm pregnant," Cassie admitted, her blue eyes not straying from his. The room seemed to hold its breath.

Andy's face paled slightly, disbelief etched momentarily across his features before giving way to a stunned silence. They sat together, letting the weight of her words settle between them.

"Are you sure?" Andy finally asked.

"Quite sure," Cassie replied, feeling a strange sense of calm now that the secret was shared.

As they sat at the wooden kitchen table, their hands found each other, grasping for comfort and reassurance amidst the uncertainty.

Cassie broke the silence first, her practical nature guiding her words. "I'm scared, Andy. What about my dressmaking? I've dreamt of that shop since I was a girl."

He listened, his thumb gently stroking her hand. "Cassie, love," he said with a soft firmness, "we'll make it work. You're the finest seamstress I know. If anyone can do it, it's you. Maybe Jane could work more hours..."

Her heart fluttered at his confidence, even as doubts nagged at her. "But a baby...this changes everything."

"Maybe it does," Andy agreed, his entrepreneurial spirit shining through. "But we'll figure it out, together. We always do." Andy rose from his chair, pacing back and forth across the creaky floorboards of their humble kitchen. "Cassie," he began, the words catching in his throat, "I never thought—well, I never allowed myself to think we'd have a child."

"Nor I," Cassie admitted, watching him with an understanding gaze.

He stopped, hands on his hips, and turned to face her. "It's just...do you reckon we're ready for this? To be parents?" The worry creased his brow, betraying his usual stoicism.

"Ready or not, it's happening," Cassie said, a wry smile touching her lips. She shook her head. "I find that I'm much more delighted with the prospect than I thought I would be."

"You're right," he conceded, chuckling despite himself. "I suppose my biggest fret is providing for you both. The ranch hasn't been turning the profits I hoped for yet."

"Then we'll tighten our belts," she replied with unwavering spirit. "We'll scrimp and save a little."

"I guess that's what families do."

"Exactly," Cassie said, her heart swelling at the sight of his growing grin. "We'll teach our child the value of hard work and dreaming big, just like us."

"Speaking of dreams," Andy said, taking a seat beside her once more, "what do you hope for our baby?"

"Health and happiness," she answered instantly. "But also...curiosity. A sense of adventure, maybe."

"Like their mother," Andy said, his dark eyes twinkling. "And a good head for business, like their father."

Cassie laughed, the sound light and free. "Let's not set the bar too high."

"High enough to reach for the stars," he insisted, his hand finding hers again. "Imagine them riding across the fields, or better yet, helping you pin patterns and sort fabrics."

"Or counting cattle and fixing fences," Cassie added. Now she had something new to dream about, and she found herself looking forward to the baby.

"Whatever they choose, we'll be there," Andy said, squeezing her hand gently.

Later, Cassie and Andy sat side by side on the porch swing, the rhythmic creak of the chains a gentle backdrop to their quiet contemplation.

"Imagine," Cassie said, "how it would be if it was just us knowing about this little miracle for a while longer."

Andy nodded, his gaze fixed on the horizon. "Yeah, just us," he agreed, his voice soft with wonder. He turned to look at her, his dark eyes reflecting a shared secret. "We'll tell everyone in good time."

She leaned into him, feeling the solidness of his presence. "Our special secret," she said with a smile.

"Special indeed." His arm came around her shoulders, pulling her closer. "So, what's next, Cassie? What do we plan for first?"

"First?" She tilted her head, considering. "I suppose we should think about adding a room. And I'll need to adjust my dress designs...for a while." The thought sparked a new kind of creativity within her.

"Room, yes," Andy mused, his practical mind already turning over the logistics. "And your dresses will be the talk of the town, as always."

They rocked gently, the swing's motion comforting as they let their imaginations roam. Thoughts of cradles and booties mingled with visions of cattle counts and fabric swatches.

"Think they'll like horses?" Andy asked suddenly, a playful glint in his eyes.

"Or needles and thread," Cassie countered with a laugh. "Maybe both."

"Could be," he said, the grin reaching his voice. "A rancher-seamstress. Or seamster?"

"Anything is possible," she whispered.

As the day stretched lazily before them, they continued to dream aloud, each idea more endearing than the last. Their plans were tentative sketches, lines drawn in the soft soil of hope, but they held the weight of a future yet to be written.

"Never thought I'd be this happy," Cassie murmured, breaking the quiet. The words floated between them like the cottonwood fluff that danced in the evening breeze.

"Neither did I," Andy admitted, his voice warm with emotion. He turned to look at her, his dark eyes reflecting the last light of day. "You've made this house a home, Cass. And now, with a little one..." His voice trailed off, awed by the enormity of it all.

Cassie lifted her gaze to meet his. "We're going to be parents," she said, wonder lacing her tone.

"Parents," he echoed, the word strange and new in reference to the two of them, but not unwelcome.

They stood up from the swing, hands clasped tightly as they walked inside their humble home. The wooden floorboards creaked underfoot, a familiar soundtrack to their lives together.

"Let's turn in early tonight," Andy suggested, his thumb stroking the back of her hand.

"Sounds perfect," Cassie agreed, the prospect of rest welcome after the day's emotional whirlwind.

In the quiet sanctuary of their home, they readied for bed with practiced ease. Andy watched as Cassie braided her blond hair, fingers working with skilled dexterity.

"Think our kid will have your talent?" he asked with a chuckle.

"Or your stubbornness," she shot back playfully.

"Hey, that's perseverance," he corrected, feigning offense.

"Sure is," she acquiesced, her lips curving into a smile.

They slipped under the quilt. As they settled in, Andy wrapped an arm around Cassie, pulling her close. Her head found its place against his chest, listening to the steady rhythm of his heart.

CASSIE STIRRED, HER dreams fading as reality gently nudged her awake. She felt Andy's arm draped over her waist, his breathing deep and even. Already, she could sense a new energy between them — a shared purpose that seemed to hum in the air like the promise of spring.

"Morning already?" Andy mumbled, his voice thick with sleep.

"Seems so," Cassie replied, her tone soft. She turned to face him, her blue eyes meeting his dark ones with a sparkle of excitement. "We've got a lot to plan for."

"Yep." He stretched lazily, the corners of his mouth lifting. "First thing's getting those new shelves started for you."

Cassie's heart swelled at his support, her fears from yesterday now distant shadows. "And we'll need to decide where to add on another room to this cabin."

"Baby steps, Cass," he chuckled, kissing her forehead. "Pun intended."

They rose, the morning routine now tinged with a fresh layer of joy. Breakfast was a simple affair, but each bite tasted like hope. As Andy left for the fields, he paused at the door, looking back at Cassie with a grin.

"Tonight, we plan for the future," he declared. "Our future."

"Can't wait," she said, her words sincere and full of possibility.

Cassie spent the day sewing as she always did, listening to Jane talk about her beaus. "Are you ever going to choose one?" Cassie asked.

Jane shrugged. "I don't know. I'll think I like one best, and then another will take me for a walk, and I'll think I like him best. I'll figure it all out eventually."

Cassie simply laughed, shaking her head. Jane would decide, but she was certainly taking her time about it.

After Jane had left that evening, Andy seemed to have nervous energy as Cassie kept stitching away, trying to meet her deadlines for finishing the dresses she was working on.

"Think it'll be a boy or a girl?" Andy asked, his curiosity childlike.

"Doesn't matter," Cassie replied. "As long as they have your kindness."

"And your strength," he countered, his admiration clear.

"Never thought I'd be this happy," she said softly, almost afraid that if she spoke too loudly it would all be taken away.

"Life's full of surprises," he said, squeezing her hand.

In the quiet that followed, there was an understanding that no words were necessary — their hearts spoke volumes.

"Goodnight, Cassie," Andy whispered as they retreated into the embrace of their home.

"Goodnight, Andy," she whispered back, her spirit soaring.

Chapter Eleven

The last echoes of Christmas carols had long since faded into the crisp winter air, and with them, the memory of Brenda's grand holiday festivities. The once bustling church, filled to the brim with laughter and the sweet scent of pine, now stood silent—a testament to the passing of another season.

"Never thought I'd miss the chaos," Cassie mused to herself, her fingers deftly pinning a hem on one of the many dresses crowding her worktable. .

But March winds brought more than just the promise of warmer days; they whispered of change. Cassie's hands rested on her swelling belly, a gentle reminder that soon, she'd have to slow her pace.

"Can't keep up like this much longer," she confided to the empty room.

It was then that Judy, a sprightly girl with nimble fingers, came bounding through the doorway, her youthful enthusiasm a stark contrast to Cassie's growing weariness.

"Morning, Cassie! What are we tackling today?" Judy asked, her eyes bright as she took in the array of fabrics and patterns strewn about.

"Good morning, Judy. We've got dresses for the Mueller wedding and Mrs. Benson's spring wardrobe," Cassie replied, guiding Judy to the sewing machine. "I'll need you to focus on the stitching while I handle the fittings."

"Sure thing!" Judy said, her feet eagerly pumping the treadle as the machine hummed to life.

In the weeks that followed, Judy proved to be an invaluable asset. She absorbed Cassie's teachings with the eagerness of a parched plant soaking up rainwater.

"Like this?" Judy asked, holding up a nearly finished sleeve for inspection.

"Exactly like that," Cassie said, a smile tugging at the corners of her mouth. Judy was an eager pupil, and Cassie was a happy teacher.

Cassie found solace in Judy's companionship. Together, they stitched and laughed, making light work.

"Miss Cassie, do you reckon we'll finish in time for the baby?" Judy inquired one day, her needle pausing mid-stitch.

Cassie glanced at the small mountain of orders yet to be fulfilled and then down at her round belly. "With you here, Judy, I believe we will."

CASSIE STOOD IN THE middle of the newly added room, a soft smile gracing her lips as she traced her fingers over the smooth wooden crib that was now situated by the window.

"Looks like we're ready for you, little one," she murmured, her hand resting gently on the swell of her belly. The child within stirred, as if in agreement, and Cassie's heart swelled with a love so profound it startled her. As much as she'd never wanted children, she had a hard time believing just how eager she was for this one to arrive.

Setting aside her client work for the day, she unfurled delicate fabrics across the sewing table—a quilt of soft pinks and blues, tiny gowns that awaited her skilled hands. As she threaded her needle, Cassie hummed a tune from her childhood, the melody carrying her through each careful stitch. Sewing for her baby was a joy unlike any commission she'd ever undertaken.

A sigh escaped her as she clipped the final thread on a petite frock adorned with lace. "If only sewing could solve all my worries," she said to the empty room. It wasn't the work itself that troubled her—it was the nagging thought that perhaps her ambition for her business might be curtailed by motherhood.

"Can I do this?" she whispered. "Have a baby and keep my shop running?"

She pictured herself juggling the roles of mother and dressmaker, the balance seeming more precarious with each passing day. Yet, as the fabric rustled beneath her fingers, she couldn't help but hope there was a way to weave together both parts of her life.

"Maybe it's possible," Cassie mused aloud, determination beginning to edge out uncertainty. "I'll find a way. For you, my sweet baby, and for me." She placed a gentle kiss atop the stack of finished baby clothes, her resolve strengthening.

"Cassie?" Judy's voice called from the doorway, tentative yet tinged with excitement. "You should come see—the roses have bloomed early this year!"

"Roses already?" Cassie stood up, easing the stiffness from her back. "Now that's a good omen if ever there was one."

CASSIE'S HANDS TREMBLED slightly as she folded a small, white gown. She set the garment aside and reached for the sturdy warmth of her teacup, seeking solace in its familiar form.

"Deborah," Cassie began, her voice soft yet carrying an undercurrent of concern, "I need to talk to you about something."

Deborah looked up from her knitting, her fingers stilling mid-stitch. "Of course, Cassie. What's on your mind?"

"It's the baby." Cassie hesitated, her blue eyes searching her sister's gentle face. "I'm scared I won't manage to keep the shop running once the little one arrives."

Deborah set her knitting aside and came to sit beside her sister, her presence like a calm harbor. "Cassie, you've built something incredible here. We all see it. And you're not alone in this."

"But how can I do both?" Cassie asked, her gaze falling to the folds of fabric in her lap.

"Let us help," Deborah replied with a serene certainty that seemed to quiet some of Cassie's fears. "We're family, and that's what families do."

IN THE DAYS THAT FOLLOWED, Deborah took action. She gathered their sisters together, each of them brimming with the kind of enthusiasm that could light up the darkest of nights.

"Girls," Deborah said, "Cassie needs us. Let's throw a party for her and the baby—a real celebration of new beginnings."

One by one, the sisters offered up their talents. Amy baked her famous pies despite Cassie's protestations—she may hate to bake, but she never said no to a slice of apple pie. Brenda's knack for organization meant invitations were sent out quicker than a jackrabbit. Erna, always the life of the party, plotted games that had everyone chuckling just at the thought.

"Judy can help me with the sewing," Cassie suggested, feeling her spirits lift with each passing moment.

"Of course she can," said Deborah. "And we'll make sure everything's perfect."

As preparations for the party unfolded, the house buzzed with the warmth of shared effort and laughter. Cassie found herself swept up in the joy, her worries easing as she saw the love her sisters poured into every detail.

"Looks like you're getting your wish," Deborah whispered to her during a quiet moment, both sisters watching as Hannah tied ribbons along the porch railings. "A family and a business."

Cassie linked her arm through Deborah's, squeezing gently. "Thanks to you all, I think I just might."

As Cassie greeted guests and accepted well-wishes, she knew that with her sisters by her side, she could indeed have it all—a family, a business, and a community that felt like home.

CASSIE STOOD IN THE doorway, her hand resting on the small swell of her belly, watching as a room once empty now brimmed with love and anticipation. The nursery was ready thanks to her sisters' tireless work during the party. Each corner held traces of their affection; a quilt sewn by Amy, stuffed animals crafted by Hannah, and a mobile of carved wooden birds that Erna had whittled during long winter evenings.

"Looks like this little one's going to be well looked after," Brenda said, gesturing around the room with a grin. Cassie's heart swelled with gratitude, her eyes misting over.

"Y'all have done so much already," Cassie replied, her voice thick with emotion.

"Stuff and nonsense," Imogene chimed in from behind, her hands firmly planted on her hips. "You're our sister, Cassie. This is what family does."

"Besides," Jane added, carrying a basket filled with colorful spools of thread, "we're not finished yet. We're all pitching in with the dresses. You'll meet your orders with time to spare."

"Really?" Cassie's eyebrows lifted in surprise.

"Absolutely," Deborah confirmed with a nod. "We've got your back, Cassie."

"Thank you," Cassie whispered, her words barely audible but heavy with sincerity.

The clatter of wood on wood drew Cassie's attention to the porch the next morning. She stepped outside, the cool March air nipping at her cheeks, to find a beautifully crafted cradle sitting right there by her doorstep. Its sturdy oak frame was polished to a shine, and atop it fluttered a sky-blue ribbon that caught the early sunlight.

Gail's handiwork, no doubt. Cassie didn't even need to see the familiar bold strokes of Gail's knife on the wood or the way the cradle was engineered to rock just right. It was all Gail—practical and made to last a lifetime.

"Isn't it just wonderful?" breathed Faith, who had come up beside her.

"It's perfect," Cassie murmured, reaching out to let the ribbon tickle her fingers. "Gail's outdone herself."

"Always does," Faith agreed with a smile.

"Tell her...tell her it's the best gift I could've received," Cassie said, knowing her words would make their way back to her sister.

"I will," Faith promised, wrapping an arm around Cassie's shoulders. "But she already knows."

As they turned back toward the house, Cassie felt a deep sense of peace settling within her. Her business, her child, her life—it was all coming together.

CASSIE SAT AT HER BELOVED sewing machine, the rhythmic hum of its needle merging with the chirping of birds outside her window. Spring was breathing new life into the world, and it seemed to be doing the same for her. As she stitched the hem of a lavender gown, her mind wandered not to the seams and fabric before her, but to the tiny life growing within her. She paused, resting a hand on her rounded belly, a smile playing on her lips.

"Slowing down might not be so bad," she mused aloud.

The door creaked open and Andy stepped in, his boots leaving traces of the ranch's earth on her clean floors. His face was drawn with the weariness of long days overseeing the birthing of calves.

"Looks like you're deep in thought," he said, leaning against the doorframe.

"Indeed. I've made a decision," Cassie replied, turning toward him, her blue eyes shining with resolve. "I'm cutting back on the dresses. Just a few each month. And...I'll be raising my prices."

Andy's dark brows raised, but his lips curled in support. "If anyone can make that work, it's you," he said.

"Thank you," she said, grateful for his unwavering faith in her. "I want to be there for our child, not lost in a sea of satin and lace."

"You will be." Andy's voice was firm, his belief in their partnership unshakable.

There was a moment of comfortable silence before he shifted, pushing off from the frame. "Speaking of being there, the calving's started. It's going to be a busy season."

"Can I help?" Cassie asked, half-rising from her chair, driven by the sense of solidarity that always filled the home.

"Stay put," he chuckled, gently pressing her back down. "Your brothers-in-law are coming. We'll manage."

"Are you certain?"

"Absolutely. It's what family does."

Within hours, the ranch was alive with activity. Men worked in unison, their figures silhouetted against the setting sun as they tended to the newest additions to their sprawling brood. From her window, Cassie watched as they moved with purpose, each one contributing to the thriving heart of the homestead.

"Seems like you've got yourself quite the team out there," Judy remarked, stepping beside Cassie with her own hands full of fabric.

"More than a team," Cassie reflected, watching Andy instruct and assist with a gentle authority. "A family."

"Big one, too," Judy added with an admiring glance outside.

"Very big," Cassie agreed, the corners of her mouth lifting into a smile. "And about to get bigger."

As dusk settled over the land, the sounds of laughter and camaraderie drifted through the air, mingling with the occasional cry of a newborn calf. The circle of life continued, and within it, Cassie found her place—not just as a dressmaker or a mother-to-be, but as a vital part of something much greater than herself.

Chapter Twelve

Cassie fidgeted with the hem of the cotton dress draped over her lap, her fingers tracing the stitches she had sewn with such precision. It was already June, and the heat was oppressive. Her heart should've been light with the joy of impending motherhood, but the closer she came to her due date, the more anxious she became.

"Can't believe it's nearly time," Andy said, his voice brimming with a kind of excitement Cassie found herself unable to share. He stood in the doorway, his dark hair tousled from work, eyes gleaming like two polished stones.

She looked up at him, biting her lip. "Andy, I need to talk to you about something important."

He walked over and knelt beside her chair, taking her hand in his rough ones. "Anything, Cassie. What's on your mind? You feeling all right?"

"It's just...what if I'm not cut out for this?" Her voice was barely above a whisper, her blue eyes searching his for understanding. "What if I don't have the motherly instinct? I've never felt a yearning for children, not like other women do."

Andy squeezed her hand and let out a chuckle, the sound meant to be reassuring. "Cassie, you worry too much. You're going to be a wonderful mother. Our child will be lucky to have you."

"But what if I see our baby and feel nothing?" The words tumbled out before she could stop them, revealing the depth of her fear.

"Impossible," he replied with a confident grin. "The moment you hold our little one, you'll be filled with love. I know it." His belief was sincere, yet it failed to help her feel any better.

"Your confidence is heartening, Andy, but..." Cassie trailed off, her hands now still in her lap.

"Look at you, Cassie. Everything you do, you do well. Remember how you turned this house into a home? Or how every dress you make becomes the talk of the whole congregation?" Andy's dark eyes were earnest, his faith in her unwavering.

"Making a dress isn't the same as raising a child," she countered softly.

"Perhaps not," he conceded, "but it's all in the care you put into it. And nobody has more care to give than you." His thumb brushed against her knuckles in a soothing rhythm.

Cassie wanted to believe him, to share in his excitement, but doubt was a stubborn companion. She forced a smile, hoping it would change how she felt, but nothing seemed to make her feel any better about the baby that was so close to making his or her entrance into the world.

"Let's not worry about tomorrow," Andy suggested, standing and offering her his hand. "Tonight, we enjoy this beautiful evening together. How about that?"

"All right," Cassie agreed, allowing him to help her to her feet. They stepped outside, and sat on the porch swing, his arm around her shoulders. If only she could be certain that her love for the baby would be as strong as her love for the baby's father.

CASSIE WAS PERCHED on the edge of the porch, her sewing basket abandoned beside her, when Amy arrived. With a baby secured in each arm and her youngest step-daughter trailing behind her, Amy's smile was as bright as Cassie had ever seen it.

"Look who's come to visit Auntie Cassie," Amy declared. Cassie marveled at how truly happy Amy seemed with the babies in her arms.

"Hi, Cassie!" Priscilla said, climbing up the steps to throw her small arms around an awkwardly seated Cassie.

"Hello, dear," Cassie replied, managing a gentle pat on the child's back. Her eyes drifted to the bundles in Amy's arms—one of the babies cooing softly, blissfully unaware of the turmoil he stirred in Cassie's heart.

"May I?" Cassie asked tentatively, indicating she wanted to hold Amy's son. As the infant was placed carefully into her arms, Cassie felt a surge of something unfamiliar—a warmth that started in her chest and spread outward. Yet, it was overshadowed by the gnawing doubt that lingered like a persistent shadow.

"Isn't he just perfect?" Amy gushed, watching Cassie with a proud maternal glow.

"Yes, he's quite...charming," Cassie agreed, though her voice lacked conviction. The baby, sensing her unease, began to fuss, and Cassie bounced him gently, more out of duty than instinct.

"Is everything all right? You seem off today," Amy said, concern knitting her brow as she reclaimed her son, expertly soothing his cries.

Cassie sighed, her blue eyes meeting Amy's dark ones. "I'm scared, Amy. What if I don't feel that...that bond when my own arrives?"

Amy chuckled, dismissing the worry with a wave of her hand. "Oh, Cassie, everyone thinks that at first. But trust me, when you see your baby, it'll be love at first sight. Just like it was for me with these two."

"Will it?" Cassie muttered, not convinced.

"Of course! Just wait and see. You're going to be a natural," Amy assured her with a confident nod.

"Perhaps," Cassie murmured, but her heart wasn't in it. She watched as Amy doted on her sons with such effortless devotion. Would that ever be me? Cassie wondered, a soft breeze ruffling her blond hair, carrying away her whispered doubts.

CASSIE'S FINGERS WERE a blur of motion as she fed fabric through the sewing machine. She was trying to focus on the dresses, vibrant calicos meant for the general store, but her mind wandered, unbidden, to the impending arrival that colored every moment with anticipation and fear.

"Stitches look even as always," Hortense observed from the doorway, her voice calm and soothing like a balm. The elderly midwife stepped into the room, her hands clasped in front of her apron, a basket of medical supplies by her side.

"Thank you, Hortense," Cassie replied, pausing her work to look at the woman who had become a pillar of strength for many mothers in the community. "I just wish my thoughts were as orderly as my stitches."

"Mind if I sit?" Hortense gestured toward a chair as Cassie nodded. There was something about Hortense's presence that made everything seem calmer, more natural.

"Every mother finds her way," Hortense said, pulling her chair closer. "Now, tell me what's weighing on your heart. I can see you're troubled by something."

Cassie hesitated. Finally, the words spilled out. "It's foolishness, I suppose. But I worry...What if I don't feel that fierce love for my baby? What if I look at him—or her—and feel nothing?" Cassie truly worried that something inside her was broken, and she would be incapable of loving the little person who God had given her.

Hortense reached out, her weathered hand covering Cassie's own. "Child, I've delivered more babies than I can count, and not one of those mothers has been unhappy with their child. Fear is natural, but it's the love that takes you by surprise."

"Really?" Cassie asked.

"Truly," Hortense smiled. "You've got so much love in you, dear. It'll come pouring out when the time is right."

Somehow, Cassie believed her. With a renewed sense of purpose, she turned back to the dresses, stitching away the last of the morning hours.

The clock ticked on, and Cassie worked, her hands moving with practiced ease. Each dress was a masterpiece of color and craft, but as the pile grew, so did her restlessness. "Should have saved some of this work for later," she muttered to herself, considering the empty days stretching before her until the baby's birth.

"Work keeps the mind steady," Hortense remarked, standing to pack her things. "But rest is just as important. Remember that, Cassie."

"I will, Hortense." Cassie felt the tightness in her chest soften just a bit. With each stitch, she felt slightly more prepared.

CASSIE'S HANDS WERE steady as she threaded a needle despite the unrest in her heart. A soft clatter of needles announced Deborah's arrival, her knitting basket in tow. Settling beside Cassie, she pulled out a half-finished shawl, the yarn a calming shade of blue.

"Remember when we'd race to see who could finish their chores first back at the home?" Deborah asked, her voice gentle as the click of her knitting needles.

Cassie chuckled. "I always lost. You had a way with those socks and gloves that I never managed."

"Yet here you are," Deborah said, glancing over at the dresses arrayed like a colorful fan across the table, "creating beauty from fabric."

"Sometimes I wonder if I'll be any good with a baby," Cassie confessed, her stitches faltering for a heartbeat.

Deborah stopped knitting, her eyes warm yet serious. "Cassie, you've excelled at everything you've put your mind to. I can't sew a perfect seam to save my life, but you—you're going to be a wonderful mother."

"Easy for you to say," Cassie sighed.

"Truly," Deborah insisted, the corners of her eyes crinkling with conviction. "And we'll all help. We've decided to bring meals for you after the baby comes."

"Every day?" Cassie blinked, the worry lines on her forehead smoothing slightly.

"Every single day," Deborah affirmed, her needles resuming their dance. "You won't have to cook unless you want to."

"Thank you," Cassie murmured, the knot in her chest loosening. The thought of her sisters' support filled her with contentment. She would have her hands full with the baby, and doing anything beyond taking care of him...well, it felt like too much.

"Anytime," Deborah said. "Now, let me see that dress. I think you dropped a stitch."

"Impossible," Cassie joked, handing over the garment with feigned indignance.

"See? Even in jest, you aim for perfection." Deborah winked, and they both laughed, the sound mingling with the hum of the summer afternoon, light-hearted and full of promise.

CASSIE'S HAND FLEW to her belly as a sharp twinge caught her by surprise. She drew in a quick breath, steadying herself against the table laden with fabric scraps and half-finished dresses. The pain subsided as quickly as it came, but Cassie knew what it signified. Her heart thumped unevenly, a mix of fear and something she couldn't quite name pulsing through her veins.

"Judy!" Cassie called out, trying to keep the tremble from her voice. "I need you!"

The screen door clattered as Judy hurried in, eyes wide and alert. "What is it, Cassie? What's wrong?"

"Fetch Hortense," Cassie instructed, gripping the edge of the table. "It's time."

"Already?" Judy's voice hitched in a mix of excitement and worry. "But I thought—"

"No time for thoughts, dear," Cassie cut in, more sharply than intended. She softened her tone, "Please, hurry."

Judy nodded, her youthful face set with determination. She dashed out, hiking her skirts up almost to her knees as she ran for the midwife.

Left alone, Cassie sank into a chair, her fingers knitting together over her swelling belly. The room seemed suddenly too quiet, too still. Cassie tried to chase away the nagging doubts that clouded the fringes of her mind. Would she really be able to love this child? Could she be the mother it deserved?

She whispered to the emptiness, "Oh, what if I'm the worst mother who has ever lived?"

There was no reply, just the distant sound of Judy's footsteps fading away. Cassie closed her eyes, taking deep, measured breaths, willing her fears to dissipate with each exhale. But they clung stubbornly, heavy as the summer heat.

"Come on, Cassandra Forsythe," she murmured to herself. "You've tackled tougher things than this."

Yet, the reassuring words felt hollow. She could sew a fine seam, whip up a meal that'd make your mouth water, but none of that seemed to matter now. This was different. This was a tiny life that would depend on her for everything.

As another contraction began its slow, building pressure, Cassie leaned back, envisioning the faces of her sisters, their smiles and assurances. They believed in her—maybe, just maybe, it was time she started believing in herself too.

"Love and companionship," she breathed out. That's what Deborah had said. With her sisters' support and a community that felt like an extended family, perhaps she could find her way. And maybe, just maybe, the love she was so afraid wouldn't come would arrive with the first cry of her newborn baby.

Chapter Thirteen

Cassie's breath came in sharp gasps as she paced the length of the house, each step measured and deliberate. The pains that gripped her were like none she'd ever known. Her blond hair, usually so neatly styled, clung to her forehead in damp tendrils.

"Lord, have mercy," she whispered between clenched teeth, her blue eyes narrowing with each wave of discomfort.

The door creaked open, and Judy, cheeks flushed from the rush, hurried in, with Hortense trailing behind her. Hortense, with her years of midwifery, cast a practiced eye over Cassie and nodded firmly.

"Judy, go fetch Andy," Hortense instructed, her voice a calm anchor in the storm of Cassie's mounting distress. "It's time."

"Right away," Judy said, the words tumbling out as she turned on her heel and darted back outside to inform Andy his child was on its way.

Alone now with Hortense, Cassie ceased her pacing and leaned heavily against the sturdy dresser, its surface littered with the implements of childbirth. She had no idea how she was going to make it through the birth of this child, but she was going to do her best to not make a fool of herself.

"Can't this baby hurry up?" Cassie huffed, trying to add humor to the situation but falling flat.

"Nature takes its course, dear," Hortense replied, preparing linens with deft hands. "You're doing just fine."

Fine felt like a foreign concept to Cassie as another contraction seized her. She grasped the edge of the dresser, her knuckles whitening. Hours slipped by, marked by the rhythmic ticking of the modest clock on the wall and Cassie's low moans.

"Never...going to end," Cassie muttered, the usual formality of her speech fraying at the edges.

"Shh, now," Hortense soothed as she supported Cassie through another wave. "Your body knows what it's doing."

As the night wore on, Cassie's resolve began to fade. Her strength ebbed, leaving her with a raw, primal urge to scream—to unleash the frustration and anticipation that swelled within her.

And scream she did, a sound that echoed off the walls and spilled out into the cool evening air.

"Let it out, Cassie," Hortense encouraged, not flinching at the display of raw emotion. "It's all right."

WITH THE FINAL PUSH, a stillness fell over the room, punctuated only by the soft cry of new life. Hortense, with practiced hands and a tender smile, wrapped the tiny baby in a homespun blanket and presented it to Cassie.

"Look what you've done," Hortense said, her voice filled with warmth as she placed the baby in Cassie's weary arms.

It was a girl—a beautiful little girl with wisps of blond hair like her mother. Cassie had been so sure she'd bear a son to take after Andy, to work alongside him on the ranch. But here she was, holding a tiny little girl, who seemed too delicate to touch.

"Hello there," Cassie whispered, her voice a pale echo of its usual surety. She took in the miniature features, searching for the overwhelming surge of love she'd been promised.

But it didn't come.

Instead, she felt a curious detachment as she studied the face that somehow mirrored her own blue eyes and Andy's dark, determined brow. A pang of guilt nestled into her chest. Wasn't a mother supposed to be consumed by love the very second she laid eyes on her child?

"Why don't I..." Cassie started, her gaze not leaving the infant's face.

"Give it time, dear," Hortense reassured, patting Cassie's hand. "Love's got a way of creeping up on you when you least expect it."

Cassie nodded, hoping the wise midwife's words would prove true. For now, she held her daughter closer, praying the emotions would come.

The door creaked open, and Andy's boots thudded softly on the wooden floor as he approached with a mix of caution and awe painted across his face. His eyes were wide with an emotion that seemed to be a mix of joy and disbelief.

"Is that...?" His voice trailed off as he came to stand beside Cassie's bed.

Cassie looked up at him, her blond hair clinging damply to her forehead. "A girl," she confirmed, her voice steadier than she felt.

Andy let out a slow breath, the corners of his mouth lifting into a tender smile. "She's beautiful," he murmured, gazing down at the tiny bundle in Cassie's arms. "Like a little daisy."

Cassie's lips twitched, a hint of her humor finding its way through the exhaustion. "Daisy, huh?" She considered the name, turning it over in her mind like a smooth stone from the creek. It was simple, sweet, and somehow fitting for the delicate life she cradled.

Andy nodded, his eyes never leaving the infant's face. "Yeah. Daisy."

"All right then. Daisy it is." Cassie agreed, feeling a flicker of partnership in the shared decision.

Then, Andy's hands reached out, his fingers gently brushing against the small swaddled form. "May I?" he asked, his voice soft as if afraid to break the tranquility of the moment.

Cassie's heart clenched tight. A sudden urge to pull Daisy back to her chest washed over her. She'd carried this child, nurtured her within her own body, and now Andy thought to just take her away? Cassie's hands tightened instinctively around Daisy, a fierce protectiveness flaring within her.

"Careful," she said, more sharply than she intended. Her gaze locked onto Andy's, silently communicating the gravity of the trust she was placing in his hands.

"Of course," Andy replied, a glimmer of understanding crossing his features. He took Daisy with a gentleness that was surprising for his sturdy rancher's hands, cradling her as if she were the most precious calf he had ever ushered into the world.

Watching them together, Cassie felt a strange tug inside her, a connection to both Andy and the child that was theirs and yet so new. She didn't have to love fiercely, not yet. But perhaps, in time, she would learn to share.

"Here you go," Andy whispered, his voice carrying the weight of awe and reverence for the life they had created.

Andy's arms, once strong and steady, trembled ever so slightly as he returned Daisy to Cassie's waiting embrace. The baby nestled back into her mother's hold with a soft sigh that seemed to echo within the quiet room. At that moment, something shifted in Cassie's heart—a warmth, a swelling of emotion she couldn't put into words but felt with an intensity that took her breath away.

"Thank you," Cassie murmured, her eyes never leaving the tiny face peeking out from the blanket. This was love—the fierce, protective kind that came from deep within, unbidden and powerful. Holding Daisy felt more natural than anything Cassie had ever done. It was as if a missing piece of her soul had finally clicked into place.

Andy rubbed the back of his neck, watching them for a moment longer before clearing his throat. "I'll get you some milk," he said, his tone attempting nonchalance though his eyes betrayed the enormity of the moment.

"All right," Cassie replied softly, her attention still fixed on Daisy.

Left alone with her daughter, Cassie traced the delicate features that were a mix of her and Andy. She leaned down, whispering promises and dreams into the tiny, curved ear. "We're going to have such fun, you and I," she cooed. "I'll teach you how to stitch the finest seams and craft gowns fit for a princess."

As she spoke, visions of sunny afternoons spent by the window with Daisy, fabrics spread around them, filled her mind. They would work together, fingers dancing over cloth, creating beauty stitch by stitch—a future as bright and full of promise as the name they had chosen for this precious girl.

Cassie's heart swelled with every tiny breath the baby took. The room was quiet but for the soft sounds of life unfurling in her arms. She marveled at how such a small thing could rearrange her entire world. A chuckle escaped her as she realized that this tiny being and the man who had fetched her milk had become her everything.

"Can't picture it anymore," Cassie murmured to Daisy, "a day without you or your pa." She brushed a fingertip over the baby's downy cheek, feeling a smile tug at her lips. Andy was right about the name. Daisy was indeed their beautiful flower.

Andy returned, glass in hand, and offered it to Cassie with a tender look. "How are my girls doing?" he asked, his voice laced with the warmth of a hearth fire.

"Better now," Cassie replied, accepting the milk with her free hand. She drank deeply, feeling the cool liquid soothe her parched throat.

Andy leaned down, his gaze lingering on Daisy's peaceful face. "She's perfect, isn't she?" His fingers brushed lightly over the baby's blanket.

"More than perfect," Cassie agreed, reluctantly shifting Daisy into her left arm to finish her milk.

"Let me put her down for just a moment," Andy suggested gently. "You need to rest too."

With the utmost care, Andy lifted Daisy from Cassie's embrace and placed her in the cradle Gail had lovingly crafted. The sight of the sturdy little bed, with its smooth, sanded edges and the faint smell of pine, brought a sense of pride to Cassie's heart. Gail might not care much for children, but her love echoed in the cradle's craftsmanship.

As Andy settled Daisy into her new sleeping place, Cassie's arms felt suddenly cold and empty. The weight of her daughter had been a comforting presence, and without it, she felt adrift. She watched, a tightness forming in her chest as Daisy yawned and snuggled into the blankets.

"Looks like she'll grow up strong," Andy said, standing up straight and looking at Cassie with a reassuring smile.

The simple, domestic scene filled the room with an atmosphere of contentment and possibility. Despite the void in her arms, Cassie knew that this was only the beginning. Life had woven a new tapestry, vibrant and enduring, with threads of love and companionship that bound them all together. It was, she realized, exactly what she had always dreamed of—even if she hadn't known it until now.

Cassie's gaze lingered on Daisy, nestled amongst the quilts. The baby's tiny fingers curled and uncurled in her sleep, a gentle rhythm that tugged at Cassie's heartstrings. With each rise and fall of Daisy's chest, Cassie felt an invisible thread weaving tighter around her own heart.

"Can't sleep?" Andy whispered as he returned to her side, his eyes soft with understanding.

"Feels strange," Cassie murmured, not taking her eyes off Daisy. "Like I'm only half here without holding her."

"Give it time," Andy soothed, resting a hand on Cassie's shoulder. "She's right there, Cass. And she's perfect."

"Thanks to you," Cassie replied, a smile breaking through her unease. Her heart swelled at his touch, a reminder of their shared love embodied in the child before them.

"Thanks to us, you mean." Andy's voice was low and warm.

"Maybe...Maybe I could just hold her a little longer?" Cassie's voice was tentative, but her need was clear.

"Sure thing." Andy's agreement was swift and gentle as he carefully lifted Daisy from the cradle and placed her back into Cassie's waiting arms.

The moment Daisy's weight settled against her, Cassie's world realigned. The room was once again complete, filled with the quiet sounds of the night and the steady breathing of her daughter. She brushed a finger over the soft down of Daisy's hair, marveling at the miracle they had created.

"See? All's right," Andy said, the corners of his eyes crinkling with a smile.

Cassie nodded, unable to speak past the lump in her throat. This was love—the fierce, protective kind that consumed her doubts and filled her with purpose. Holding Daisy, feeling her warmth, sensing the rise and fall of her tiny breaths, Cassie knew she would do anything for this child. She had never been more certain of anything in her life.

"Forever, then," Cassie whispered to Daisy, her voice barely audible. "I'll hold you forever, my little love."

And in that moment, Cassie understood the true depth of love and companionship that had blossomed in her heart for her family.

Chapter Fourteen

Cassie stood at the stove, stirring a pot of stew when the door creaked open, and Deborah stepped into the warm kitchen, a smile on her face and a small bundle in her hands.

"Evening, Cassie," Deborah said.

"Deborah!" Cassie's eyes lit up, abandoning the stew for a moment to greet her sister with an embrace. "What brings you here?"

"Can't I visit my new niece?" Deborah teased, revealing the tiny knitted booties in her hands. "Made these for little Daisy."

Cassie took the booties, running a finger over the delicate stitches. "These are beautiful, Deb. Thank you." She placed them beside the cradle where Daisy lay cooing, snug in a blanket.

"Seems like you were born for this," Deborah remarked, watching as Cassie smiled down at her daughter.

"Hardly," Cassie chuckled. "But I'm learning."

From his spot by the fireplace, Andy watched the exchange, a quiet yearning etched in his gaze. He longed to scoop Daisy up, to feel her tiny heartbeat against his chest, but Cassie always seemed to be one step ahead, her arms ready to catch any whimper or fuss.

"Want to hold her?" Cassie asked, glancing back at Andy with an unreadable expression.

"Sure," he replied, though the hesitation in her offer didn't escape him.

As Cassie carefully lifted Daisy and passed her to Andy, the baby's small hand wrapped around his finger—a grip so strong it surprised him every time. Her warmth settled against his forearm, and for a moment, everything felt perfect.

"Looks like she's taken to you just fine," Deborah commented, a knowing smile gracing her lips.

Andy nodded, but the joy of holding his daughter was tinged with a faint sadness. Cassie hovered close by, as if ready to reclaim Daisy at the slightest peep. He wished she would trust him more, let him share in these moments.

"Reckon I'll get the hang of it eventually," Andy said, hoping his smile reached his eyes.

"Of course, you will," Cassie assured him, though she stepped forward to adjust the blanket around Daisy, her fingers lingering near her child.

"Suppose I better get back," Deborah said, standing. "You two take care now."

"Thanks again, Deb," Cassie called out as her sister left, closing the door gently behind her.

With Deborah gone, the room fell into a comfortable silence, broken only by Daisy's contented gurgles. Andy handed the baby back to Cassie, their fingers brushing in the exchange.

"Let's get you fed," Cassie murmured to Daisy, her gaze softening as she looked down at her daughter. Andy watched them, a silent promise forming in his heart to do whatever it took to keep that look of love on Cassie's face.

Cassie rocked back and forth in the creaky wooden chair, Daisy cradled close to her chest.

"Never thought it'd be like this," Cassie said, breaking the silence.

Andy turned, his dark eyes finding hers. "Like what?"

"Love," she whispered, her blue eyes fixed on their daughter's peaceful face. "I never knew I could feel so much for someone. For both of you."

A quiet understanding flickered across Andy's features. He walked over and knelt beside her, his hand reaching out to gently stroke Daisy's downy head.

"I know exactly what you mean," he said, his voice low and steady. "And I'm mighty glad you don't regret this—our baby, our life together."

Cassie met his gaze, a warmth spreading through her that had little to do with the fire. "Regret? Never. Not when I've got you and this little one." Her smile was soft but full of certainty, a testament to the bond they shared.

Andy grinned back, the lines around his eyes crinkling with genuine contentment. "That's good to hear, Cassie. Because I love you more than I ever thought possible."

CASSIE ROCKED GENTLY in the wooden chair, her gaze lingering on the cradle where Daisy lay sleeping. The rhythmic creak of the chair filled the room. She glanced up as Andy walked through the door.

Andy pulled another chair close, their knees almost touching. "How's our little lady tonight?"

"Sleeping like a lamb," she said, a chuckle escaping her lips.

"Good, good." Andy leaned back, his hands clasping behind his neck. "What's on your mind, Cass?"

Cassie hesitated, tracing the grain of the wood with her finger. "Andy, I've been thinking...about my sewing."

"Uh-huh?" He tilted his head, listening.

"I love making dresses, you know that," she started, her eyes not leaving the cradle. "But Daisy, she needs me."

"Of course, she does," he agreed softly.

"So, I'm thinking...maybe I should take just a few special orders. That way, I can sew when I find the time, but mostly, I'll be here for her."

Andy nodded slowly. "Sounds sensible. You should do what feels right for you and Daisy."

"Really?" A wave of relief washed over her.

"Absolutely." He reached out, covering her hand with his. "We'll manage. Might even be a blessing in disguise, gives you more time to enjoy her growing up."

Cassie's heart swelled at his support. "And what about the ranch? We still need to make ends meet."

"Ah, the ranch..." Andy's eyes gleamed with determination. "I've been turning things over in my head. I think we can expand the herd next spring, maybe even break some new land for grazing."

"Can we afford it?" Cassie asked.

"Sure we can." His confidence was infectious. "We tighten our belts a bit, and I'll work dawn till dusk if I have to. We'll make it work, Cass."

He watched as Cassie picked the baby up from her cradle, nuzzling her cheek.

"Hard to believe it's been a week already," Andy said, his eyes fixed on the tiny bundle of life that had so completely changed their world.

"Time flies when you're knee-deep in diapers and feedings," Cassie replied, a hint of mirth in her voice.

"Speaking of time flying..." Andy said. "Do you ever think about having more? Babies, I mean."

Cassie paused, considering the question as she gazed down at Daisy, whose little hand now clutched one of Cassie's fingers. "I love her more than I ever thought possible," she confessed. "And if more babies meant more of this kind of love..." Her voice trailed off, filled with wonder.

Andy chuckled. "She sure has cast a spell on us, hasn't she?"

"Spell or not, I'd be just as happy if it's only Daisy we're blessed with," Cassie said, her blue eyes lifting to meet Andy's gaze. "Because honestly, how do you improve on perfection?"

"Well, I think we could try our hand at it," Andy teased, winking. "Or we could count our blessings every single day with this little lady."

"Either way," Cassie replied, her heart light and full, "we've got everything we need right here."

Epilogue

Sunlight streamed through the open window of the cozy workshop, where bolts of fabric in various hues were neatly stacked along the walls. A gentle breeze carried the sound of laughter as Cassie carefully threaded her needle. Daisy was outside, playing with the tireless energy only a five-year-old possessed. She watched her daughter through the window, her heart swelling with a love that was both fierce and tender.

"Mama, look!" Daisy's voice floated in as she held up a wildflower crown, her blond hair catching the sun's rays like spun gold.

"Beautiful, sweet pea," Cassie called back, her hands not missing a stitch as she worked on a special order dress. Every so often, her gaze would drift back to Daisy, ensuring her little one was safe and happy.

"Careful now, don't go chasing the chickens again," she said with a light-hearted chuckle.

"I won't!" Daisy promised, skipping about with a carefree spirit that filled the home with joy.

Cassie returned to her sewing, the rhythmic hum of the machine blending with the sounds of nature. Her days were full, splitting time between her cherished role as a mother and her passion for dressmaking.

CASSIE STEPPED ONTO the porch, a glass of cool lemonade in her hand. Andy was leaning against the railing, his gaze fixed on the horizon where their land stretched out before them.

"Beautiful evening," Cassie said, taking a spot beside him, her voice soft but filled with contentment.

"Every evening's beautiful with you and Daisy around." Andy turned to her, the corners of his eyes crinkling with warmth.

Cassie sipped her drink, watching their daughter chase the dog around the yard, her laughter mingling with the rustle of the wind through the grass. She leaned into Andy, her head resting lightly against his shoulder.

"I can't imagine a more perfect life," she murmured, the truth of her words resonating deep within her heart.

Andy wrapped an arm around her waist, pulling her closer. "I feel the same way," he replied. "The ranch is doing better than I ever dreamed. Got five good men working for us now."

"Your hard work is paying off," Cassie said, pride lacing her tone as she thought about the thriving expanse they called home.

"Couldn't have done it without you, Cass. You've got a way of making everything...right." His dark eyes met hers, honest and full of love.

She smiled up at him, the simplicity of their life together filling her with an immense sense of gratitude. "As long as we have each other, that's all that matters."

"Forever and always," Andy affirmed, sealing their quiet moment with a tender kiss against her forehead.

CASSIE HUMMED A CHEERFUL tune as she threaded the needle with practiced ease, her hands moving deftly over the rich fabric stretched out on the table before her. Sunlight filtered through the window of the cozy room that served as both her workspace and sanctuary. The walls were adorned with dress designs and sketches.

"Looks lovely, Cassie," Judy said, eyeing the elegant gown taking shape under Cassie's skilled fingers. "Mrs. Henderson will be pleased."

"Thank you, Judy." Cassie glanced up with a smile, her blue eyes sparkling. "I'm glad I've got you here to help me keep track of all these orders."

"Wouldn't want to be anywhere else," Judy replied, her voice warm with genuine affection.

The two women worked in comfortable silence, the only sounds the rhythmic snip of scissors and the occasional clink of pins into a cushion. They had developed a rhythm over the years, their partnership seamless as they crafted beautiful garments for the ladies of the town.

As the afternoon waned, Cassie stepped back from her work, stretching her arms above her head. She surveyed the fruits of their labor with satisfaction. Her dream of being a dressmaker had not only been realized but had flourished, thanks in no small part to Judy's unwavering support.

"Time to call it a day?" Judy asked, glancing at the clock on the wall.

"Yes," Cassie agreed, folding the dress carefully and setting it aside. "Daisy will be home from school soon."

"Can't keep that little one waiting," Judy chuckled, tidying up their workspace.

Soon, the sound of laughter and the patter of small feet announced Daisy's return. Cassie's heart swelled at the sight of her daughter, her blond hair a mirror of her own, her face lit with the boundless joy of childhood.

"Mama!" Daisy exclaimed, throwing herself into Cassie's open arms.

"Hello, my angel," Cassie said, lifting her daughter into a hug. "Did you have a good day?"

"The best! Miss Thompson said my reading's getting better!"

"That's wonderful, darling." Cassie set her down and ruffled her hair affectionately.

"Supper won't be long," Judy called out from the kitchen, where she'd moved to start the evening meal.

"Can I help, Miss Judy?" Daisy offered eagerly, always ready to be involved.

"Sure thing, Daisy," Judy responded, her tone inviting.

Cassie watched them for a moment, a contented sigh escaping her lips. Her life was a tapestry woven with love, companionship, and the quiet satisfaction of days well spent. Outside, the rugged beauty of the ranch stretched out beneath the wide Montana sky, while inside, her heart brimmed with a peace that whispered of home.

"Everything all right, Cass?" Andy's voice came from behind her.

"Everything's perfect," Cassie replied, turning to him with a smile that said more than words ever could. "Absolutely perfect."